THE DIAMOND EMPIRE

ALSO BY K'WAN

THE DIAMOND EMPIRE

K'WAN

St. Martin's Griffin
New York

THE DIAMOND EMPIRE. Copyright © 2017 by K'wan. All rights reserved. Printed in the United States of America. For information, address St. Martin's Press, 175 Fifth Avenue, New York, N.Y. 10010.

www.stmartins.com

Designed by Omar Chapa

The Library of Congress Cataloging-in-Publication Data is available upon request.

ISBN 978-1-250-10263-8 (trade paperback)
ISBN 978-1-250-10264-5 (ebook)

Our books may be purchased in bulk for promotional, educational, or business use. Please contact your local bookseller or the Macmillan Corporate and Premium Sales Department at 1-800-221-7945, extension 5442, or by email at MacmillanSpecialMarkets@macmillan.com.

First Edition: October 2017

10 9 8

THE DIAMOND EMPIRE

PROLOGUE

Domo was awakened by the soft sound of music playing. He cracked one tired eye and looked for the radio to turn it off, but to his surprise it wasn't on. Curious, he sat up on the bed and looked around.

Near the window, he found Vita sitting on a stool in front of the bedroom window. The rising sun painted her naked brown body in a soft glow that made her look radiant. Pressed to her lips was her ever-faithful brass horn. Her petite fingers moved up and down the buttons, changing the pitch. Domo had become accustomed to her playing the instrument and was familiar with some of the tunes, but this one he had never heard. Something about it made his heart heavy, though he wasn't sure why.

He slid out of bed and approached Vita. Her eyes shifting was the only acknowledgment that she knew he now was standing behind her. When he draped his arms around her, the pitch changed again . . . deeper, darker. Domo could almost feel her pain pushing through the wide bell. He hugged her a little tighter and nestled his cheek to hers. "You okay, ma?"

Vita removed the horn from her lips. "I'm fine," she said, patting his cheek affectionately.

"Then why were you playing that sad-ass song?" Domo asked. It was then he noticed a tear sparkling in the corner of her eye. "What's the matter, V? Didn't I hit it good enough?"

Vita smiled. "Nah, you hit it too good. You're a quick study."

"I got a great teacher," Domo replied. "So, if it ain't the sex, what's eating at you? It's Diamonds, isn't it?"

Vita was silent.

"I should have known." Domo walked back toward the bed and snatched his boxers from the pile of clothes on the floor.

"Where are you going?" Vita slid off the stool.

"I'm out, yo. I ain't for this shit." He slipped one leg into his jeans.

"Knock it off, Domonique," Vita told him.

"No, you knock it off, *LaVita*," Domo shot back. "Shorty, I like you a lot, but ain't no way this shit is gonna work if I gotta keep competing with a ghost."

"You ain't gotta compete with nobody, Domo. It's just that . . . I don't know. I'd be lying if I said Diamonds' disappearance wasn't part of it, but that ain't the only thing troubling me. Maybe I'm just having a hard time adjusting to the new order of things with Buda in charge," she admitted. It had been the elephant in the room among all of them since he had assumed control.

"You ain't the only one, ma. I hated working with Diamonds, but I think I hate working for Buda even more. Diamonds was a dick, but he wore his bullshit on his sleeve. At least I knew what to expect with him, but this Buda character . . ." Domo shook his head. "I don't like him and I don't trust him."

"Then why do you stay? You ain't took the oath yet, so you ain't bound by the code."

"Because of you!" Domo said as if the answer to the question should've been obvious.

Vita raised an eyebrow. "Don't bullshit me, Domo. You seen more money on the few jobs you've done with this crew than you would've stealing cars in Newark for an entire year."

"I can't front, y'all done put hella paper in my pocket, but money ain't never moved a nigga like me. I been broke most my life so I'm used to living without. Still, money comes a close second to what I feel when I'm around you. It almost feels like your pussy got me under some kind of spell," he joked.

"Maybe it does." Vita kissed him playfully. She was about to suggest they go another round when her cell phone rang. As Vita stood in the corner speaking in hushed tones to someone on the other end, Domo glared at her, wondering who the hell would be calling at that hour. When she ended the call, Vita answered the question on his face. "Get your gear, pretty boy. It's time to go to work."

The two lovers dressed hurriedly and started for the door. Vita felt bad about lying to Domo, but it was a necessary evil. Diamonds had been on her mind since he up and vanished. She was with Domo now, and planned to stay true to him, but it didn't stop her from wondering about her former lover. Honesty would've probably been best, but she knew a boy as young as Domo would never be able to understand the bond she and Diamonds shared and why it was so hard to purge him from her system completely. Maybe Buda was right in suggesting that Diamonds had been killed by the Stone family, but until she saw a corpse with her own eyes she knew her heart would never have closure.

PART

BORN ON THE BAYOU

LOUISIANA, 1998

BOOM! The retort of a shotgun cut through the quiet afternoon. A small flock of herons that had been sunning themselves on a path of damp mud flapped off on nervous wings a split second before two young boys came spilling from the bushes. One was a tall, lean youth of about eleven, whose thick Afro was so nappy that it had started to lock up due to neglect. His bare feet left smeared prints in the mud as he pulled the second boy along behind him. This one was shorter and on the chunky side, with a face that bore a striking resemblance to that of the first boy, only his skin was lighter.

"*Prese*, Goldie!" The taller boy urged his younger brother, trying to help him keep pace without losing his own balance.

"I can't, Diamonds." Goldie collapsed to his knees, breathing heavily from exhaustion. His legs were cramping and his heart thudded in his chest so hard that he feared it would leap clean from his body. "Maybe if we just explain to them why we did it they'll give us a break and let us go."

Diamonds spared a nervous glance back in the direction they

had just come. There was no sign of their pursuers, but he could still hear the baying of the bloodhounds drawing ever closer. It was only a matter of time before they were overrun. "Boy," he gave Goldie a serious look, "the only thing gonna break today is our necks if them crackers catch us! I'd gladly die for you, baby brother, but not if I don't have to. So, get your ass up and move!"

The sharp edge of fear in his brother's tone was enough to get Goldie back on his feet and moving.

They hadn't made it very far before the hounds came charging out of the bushes. They were massive brown creatures with sagging jowls and drooping, bloodshot eyes. Trailing them were three men dressed in fatigues and brandishing weapons. One of them twirled rope over his head like a cowboy. Diamonds held no illusions as to what the man planned to do with the noose if they were caught. When the hounds spotted the two boys they howled triumphantly, knowing that the game was almost over.

"This way." Diamonds pulled Goldie, leading him toward a stand of old willow trees a few yards away. They were withered and hunched over each other, forming a dome over the small dirt path that stretched between their rotting branches.

The moment the brothers crossed into the trees it seemed to go from day to night. The branches that hung overhead almost completely blocked out the sun, casting the path in heavy shadows and silence. With the near-complete absence of any outside noises, it was like the path existed in a world beyond the rest of the swamp.

Goldie tensed as a phantom wind crept across his neck. He looked around nervously and when his eyes landed on the glyphs carved into the bark of several of the trees he realized why his stomach was doing cartwheels. "Do you know where we are, Diamonds?" he asked, louder than he needed to.

"Yes, and so will they if you don't shut that mouth of yours!" Diamonds hissed.

They had crossed into a small patch of the swamp that the locals called Tit du Diable—"the Devil's Tit." According to local lore the Tit served as the Louisiana Bayou and the world of the unexplained. It was one of the most widely spread myths of the bayou. No one could say for sure if there was any truth to the stories about the magic and the monsters that dwelled beyond the Tit because only the foolish or the desperate ventured that deep into the swamp. Diamonds fell into the latter category.

"Baby brother," Diamonds softened his tone. "You know I'd lay down my life before I let anything touch you, be it a man or a monster. I need you to get your head off them ghost stories and your ass up this tree, unless we find ourselves swinging from one of them." He bent down, locking his fingers to form a step to help Goldie reach one of the branches.

Getting Goldie into the tree was a struggle, to say the least. It took his chubby fingers several tries before they were able to grip a branch that would hold his weight. He smiled proudly, and when he turned to tell his brother of his accomplishment the smile melted from his face. He opened his mouth to shout a warning to Diamonds, but the hound was already lunging.

When the dog collided with Diamonds, he lost his grip on his brother's foot and sent the boy swaying helplessly on the branch. Diamonds raised his arm just in time to receive the hound's teeth, which were aimed at his throat. Pain shot threw his forearm as the canine clamped down and began shaking its head violently from side to side.

"Get him, boy! You cripple that coon!" One of the fatigue-clad white men cheered the dog as it mauled Diamonds' arm.

The hound had managed to wrestle Diamonds to the ground. His arm had gone numb, and he was having a hard time moving his fingers. He was putting up a good fight, but the dog would soon win out. A shriek a few feet away drew Diamonds' attention from the dog snacking on his limb. Goldie had fallen out of the tree and was now at the mercy of the other two hounds. One was shaking his leg, while the other was trying to circle around to get at his face. Goldie fought as long as he could, but the hound was eventually successful in breaching his defenses. Diamonds looked on in horror as the canine sank its fangs into his little brother's throat.

"No!" Diamonds cried out. He grunted, and managed to squirm from under the dog and come up with his free arm around its neck. Twisting with everything he had, he snapped the dog's vertebrae. The hound was still and Diamonds was free. He made a dash for his brother to get the dogs off him, but he was tackled by two of the white men.

"Oh no, you gonna watch this here, boy!" One of the men snickered. He forced Diamonds' head into the dirt and made him watch while the hound ravaged his brother's throat. Goldie's leg flapped like a fish out of water for a few seconds and eventually went still.

Watching his baby brother's still body filled Diamonds with something so deep and heavy that grief didn't even come close to summing it up. In all his life he had never broken a promise to his baby brother until that moment, and it was the most important promise of all: never to let harm befall him. Diamonds felt so defeated that he didn't even fight when the hunters pulled him to his feet and dragged him over to a nearby tree. He never even batted an eye when they threw one end of a rope over the tree branch and secured the other around his neck. All he could do was stare at his brother's prone body in disbelief.

"Don't worry, you're gonna join your friend soon enough." The lead hunter, and probably the cruelest of the lot, tightened the noose around Diamonds' neck. "We gonna show you how we do thieves in this parish."

Diamonds gasped when the rope tightened around his neck and he felt them begin to pull him off the ground. They raised him just enough so that his tiptoes could scrape the ground, but he couldn't plant his feet to save himself. Diamonds clawed at the constricting rope around his neck, but couldn't get his fingers between his throat and the noose. It was over for him and he knew it. As he swung from the rope taking what was sure to be his last breaths, he looked around at the faces of the assembled white men and buried them into his brain. In that life or the next he would settle up with them.

Suddenly the wind picked up. It started as a breeze but quickly turned into a strong gust. It was like a storm had magically appeared within the stand of trees. Diamonds' body swung back and forth until it finally became too much and the branch holding him snapped, dropping him to the dirt and dazing him.

In the center of the clearing, not far from where Diamonds fell, a woman appeared. She was older, with deeply dark skin and silver hair poking from beneath the multicolored head scarf she sported. She leaned heavily on a wooden walking stick and glared at the men with cloudy gray eyes. When she spoke, her voice seemed to resonate throughout the stand of trees.

"I don't recall inviting any of you onto my property, so I'd thank you to take your asses and whatever your squabbles are off it."

Some of the hunters took a cautious step back, but the leader stood tall and defiant. "Old crone, I'd advise you to get your black ass back to where you came from before you get a taste of what this boy' gonna get."

The old woman laughed and when she did the wind picked up again. She took patient steps toward them, leaving small holes in the damp earth wherever her walking stick planted itself. "You think you some kinda big man out here hunting down children for sport. Maybe it's you who needs to get a taste of what you're dishing out."

The lead hunter sucked his teeth. "I've had about enough of this shit. Go get her, boys!" he ordered the hounds, but to his surprise they didn't move. "Didn't you hear what I said? Get that bitch!" The hounds still refused to move.

"If you want somebody, even an animal to do something for you, then you should try asking them nicely." The old woman cackled. She knelt in the mud and whispered something that only the hounds seemed to be able to hear because they became very agitated.

The hunters looked on in shock as the dogs began to howl loudly, running around in circles chasing their own tales. When the lead hunter reached in to try and rein in the hound closest to him, it turned and snapped at him.

"What the fuck?" He recoiled, examining his fingers to make sure they were all still accounted for.

"A taste of your own madness." The old woman sneered, revealing two gold teeth in the top of her mouth. "Let's see how the hunter likes becoming the hunted." She pointed her walking stick at the lead hunter.

All three of the hounds responded to the old woman's silent command and jumped on the lead hunter. They ripped him to pieces while his friends looked on helplessly. When the hounds turned their maddened eyes to the rest of the hunting party, the men wisely took off running, with the dogs on their heels.

"Get your cowardly assess out of my swamp!" the old woman called after them. "And you let it be known far and wide that there will be no hunting of little black boys on Auntie's land! Not now, and not ever!"

Auntie stood there for a time, waiting until the hunters were out of sight before turning her attention back to the boy who she had saved from hanging. She found him hunched over the body of a chubbier boy, sobbing heavily.

"*Réveille-toi, petit frère, réveille-toi.*" Diamonds nudged his brother, pleading for him to wake up. Goldie remained still, save for his chest rising and falling slowly. He was near the end.

Auntie approached them and shook her head sadly. "A shame when one so young is taken from the world before his time."

"Don't say that, he ain't dead!" Diamonds snapped. He was beside himself with grief.

Auntie eyed Goldie. "Maybe not yet, but he ain't long for this world, sugah. Best you can do is get him to higher ground so the scavengers can't have their way with his remains. At least he can pass into the afterlife whole." She turned to walk away, but Diamonds' voice stopped her.

"I know who you are," he called after her. "You're the Blood Witch of the Bayou, the one they call Auntie." He had heard tales of the old woman who lived at the edge of the Tit, and sometimes helped those in need, but had thought her just another myth.

Auntie chuckled, causing the leaves on the trees to sway slightly. "I whip up herbal potions for the sick and solutions for those who been wronged and can't help themselves, but that hardly qualifies me as a witch. Best I can do is brew you up some poppy for his pain so that transition isn't so bad, but outside of that I ain't sure what you want from me."

"That ain't my *friend,* he's my little brother and I want you to save him," Diamonds shot back. His voice was as desperate as his eyes when he looked at her. He stood and brushed the mud free of his knees before approaching her.

Auntie raised her walking stick and pointed it menacingly at Diamonds. "Tread lightly, child."

Diamonds paused and raised his hands submissively. "I mean you no disrespect or harm, madame." He had taken some of the bass out of his voice. "They say that your words carry enough favor with the Horseman to where you can persuade him to turn back from a soul he comes to collect. I'd do anything if you can see fit to have him give my little brother a pass," he pleaded.

Auntie snorted. "Them tales are just old backwater foolishness. Even if I did have say in such things, brokering with the Horseman can be messy business and ain't no guarantee your brother will come back the same way you remembered him when he passed. Crossing that veil changes the best of us. Sometimes they come back men and sometimes monsters." She shrugged her frail shoulders. "No matter the outcome, the retainer still has to be paid. Now that you know what's at stake, you still wanna play this game?" She eyed him.

Diamonds replied, from Goldie's bloodied body back to Auntie, *"Oui."*

Every bit of common sense she had told her to banish the young man and his troubles from her property, but the mother in her gave her pause. In his eyes, she saw not only greatness, but someone who could possibly pick up the burden she'd been carrying for nearly five decades. "So be it." She extended a withered hand.

When Diamonds took her hand, he found it cold and rough. Gnarled fingers clamped down over his and yanked him to her. He tried to pull away, but her grip was surprisingly stronger than he had expected. From somewhere within the folds of her tattered duster she produced a dagger. The handle was carved from bone and the sleek blade was black and scorched.

"What are you doing?" He continued to struggle futilely.

"This is a game of souls you're looking to play with the Horseman, little one. To sit at the table, you must first have something to wager!" she hissed before bringing the dagger down.

UNKNOWN LOCATION, 2006

Diamonds was snatched from his sleep by the scream that had forced its way from his throat. His heart boomed thunderously in his ears, and his lungs seemed to be working overtime to process oxygen. Instinctively the fingers of his left hand went to the palm of his right, expecting to find a bleeding gash, but instead found traces of the long-healed scar that Auntie had given him nearly a decade prior. The scar marked the start of his walk down the dark road that had eventually led him to the predicament he now found himself in: stretched out on a tattered cot and the prisoner of a man he had already killed . . . or so he'd thought.

"Glad to see you haven't checked out on us yet," a voice said from somewhere in the darkened room.

The fact that he wasn't alone startled Diamonds. He missed him on the first sweep of the room, but was able to pick him out on the second . . . if a *him* is what you could call it. The speaker appeared to be little more than a pair of youthful, yet seasoned, eyes staring at him from the inky haze of whatever hellhole he was in.

"For a while I thought we were going to lose you," the shadow continued.

"Sorry to disappoint you," Diamonds capped and tried to get up from the cot. An intense pain shot through his midsection and stole his breath. The room swam and he felt himself falling.

The shadow moved soundlessly and caught Diamonds before his skull could make contact with the ground. "Easy, my man. You in and out of it for the last couple of days." He helped Diamonds back to the bed. Now in the light Diamonds could get a better look at him. He was a young dude with a wavy fade, dressed in a sleek black suit, white shirt, and black tie. "You might wanna take it easy before you bust them stitches again."

"Stitches?" Diamonds didn't understand. His eyes looked down toward his naked torso and for the first time he noticed the blood-stained bandage roughly taped over his stomach. With a wince, he peeled the covering back to examine himself and was overwhelmed by the stench. The bandage smelled of the grave and so did he. Upon closer inspection, he could make out several deep gashes across his stomach. Someone had tried to stitch them closed, but they were still seeping blood and pus. It was then that the torture session with Slim came back to him. His old enemy had taken his time cutting into Diamonds with the same black dagger he had used on so many people. As promised, Slim wanted him to suffer before he died and suffering he was.

"I treated you as best I could, but my resources here are pretty limited," the young man continued. "I was able to tighten you up enough so that you don't bleed out, but I might've been too late to stop any infection. I tried to tell Slim that you need a real doctor, but as you can imagine he wasn't too keen on that idea."

Diamonds snorted. "I'll bet. Appreciate the effort, friend, but won't no modern medicine fix what's going on inside me." He gently pressed the bandage back over the wound. What he knew, but the young man didn't, was that the blade of the black dagger that had cut him was cured with a toxin that only a few knew the origins of. A simple nick could inflict pain and even sickness, not unlike the bite of a snake, but if the cut was deep enough it would bring on the Three. First came the fever, followed by madness, and when the poison finally made its way to the victim's heart it would bring about a slow, and incredibly painful, end. Over the years Diamonds had developed a tolerance to the poison, but he wasn't completely immune. If left untreated he would eventually succumb to the Three. Outside of him, only two other people knew how to make the antidote and one of them was dead by his hand.

Thinking of Auntie, Diamonds reached for the pouch that

always hung around. With a fright he realized that it was gone. Ignoring the burning of his wounds he began searching the cot and the floor around it.

"Looking for this?" The young man held up a leather cord. He examined the pouch swinging from the end of it. "Slim tossed it out with the rest of your bloody shit, but I salvaged it from the trash." He tossed it to Diamonds.

Diamonds caught the pouch and opened it, exposing the contents. It was packed with earth from the Devil's Tit, a gift from his one-time mentor and eventual victim Auntie. She had promised him that so long as he kept the soil close to his heart, Louisiana would never let him die, and up to that point it had held up its end of the bargain. He dipped his fingers into the soil and applied a small amount to his wounds. He could feel the burning recede, but it was only a temporary fix. Diamonds knew it would take more than an old woman's hex and a handful of dirt to save him from the poison that would soon ravage his body.

"You always go Dumpster diving for your captives?" Diamonds asked.

"You ain't my *captive,* you're my *charge,*" the young man corrected him. "And to answer your question, hell no. Quamdiu vobis custodiante te et custodiat in eam fidem. 'So long as you keep the faith, it shall keep you.' Even a man on death row is allowed a Bible to bring him comfort during his walk to the gas chamber, so I saw no reason to deny you a token of whatever God you worship."

"You a religious man?"

The young man thought on it. "No, just someone who respects the faith, even ones I don't follow."

Diamonds nodded in a way of thanks. "So, how long have I been here?" He was trying to calculate how much time he had before he reached the point of no return for the antidote to the blade's venom.

The young man thought on the question. "I can't say for sure. I only arrived two nights ago, but from the looks of the bruises that have started to heal already I'd say they been working you over for at least a few days."

This shocked Diamonds. It seemed like only a few hours ago Big Slim's boys had gotten the drop on him and kidnapped him from his building. If the poison had already been in his system that long, then the situation was far direr than he expected. His tolerance would allow him to hold out longer than most, but he reasoned he didn't have more than a week, maybe two if fate smiled on him. By then Big Slim killing him would be considered a mercy.

"You must've done some scandalous shit for Big Slim to opt to torture you instead of killing you outright," the young man said.

Diamonds shrugged. "Some people can't take a joke. While we being all chatty, why don't you tell me why one of Big Slim's lackeys is so concerned with my well-being? Them other two jokers seemed to take great pride in my pain."

The young man laughed. "Unnecessary cruelty is for the weak and insecure; I'm neither. Furthermore, I'm not now nor have I ever been anyone's lackey. I was simply paid to perform two tasks: to keep you alive and confined to this room."

"If Slim only saw fit to leave you to guard me he's either forgotten how I get down, or you're one bad muthafucka," Diamonds said.

"My brother, with what Slim and his boys have put you through

I doubt you could even stand on your own let alone give me any trouble. However, I didn't get this far in life by underestimating my opponents." The young man opened his suit jacket and showed Diamonds the black gun hanging from his shoulder holster. "I think it'd be in both our best interests for you to be easy and not give me any trouble, Diamonds."

Diamonds raised an eyebrow. "I'm afraid you have me at a disadvantage, *mon ami*. You know my name, but I'm afraid I don't know yours."

"And you don't need to know it, considering we're on two different sides of the gun here. But in the spirit of all this gentlemanly courtesy we've been showing each other, I'm called Brother Minister."

CHAPTER ONE

"I don't know about this, kid. Maybe we should wait until the sun goes down," Hank said from his position behind the wheel. He was an older, brown-skinned man with hard eyes and a generally sour disposition. At one time, he had been the voice of reason and wisdom of the crew, but lately his advice had fallen on deaf ears. It was a new day and they were under a new regime.

"Ordinarily I'd agree with you, old head, but timing is key on this one. We wanna make sure everybody gets the memo around the same time." This was Goldie. He was a lanky youth, with a thick goatee and hair that he wore braided into long plaits. As usual, his signature black bandanna was tied snugly around his neck. At just shy of twenty, Goldie had the combat seasoning of a man who had lived twice as long, and he was calling the shots.

"Fuck all this debate shit. I'm ready to jump out and dump on a nigga!" Snake fumed from his position in the backseat of the vehicle. He was pole thin with dark eyes and spoke with a lisp. Some thought he got his nickname because of his speech impediment, but in reality, it was because he couldn't be trusted. Snake was only loyal to whoever was holding the biggest bag, which is why Goldie couldn't understand why Buda had been so insistent on Snake going along on the mission. Lately Buda had been making quite a few suspect decisions, but he was chief of their crew now and Goldie, like the others who had taken the pirate oath, were bound by honor to follow their chief . . . at least until he gave them a reason not to.

Goldie turned in his seat and gave Snake an irritated look. "You'll get your taste of blood, killer. But only when the time is right and not a minute sooner. So cool the fuck out."

"There he is." Hank's voice broke the tension between the other two men. His eyes were fixed on a man who was coming out of the building across the street. His name was Pat Williams. Pat didn't look like much, wearing a pair of blue jeans, a New York Giants sweatshirt, and carrying a beat-up knapsack, but in the game they played looks could often be deceiving. The man was a runner for a big-time dealer named Big Stone, and strapped to his back were five kilos of uncut cocaine.

"Make a U-turn and pull up on this nigga," Goldie ordered Hank, while checking the clip of his gun.

"That's what the fuck I'm talking about," Snake said excitedly. He had only been in New York for a few days and had been itching to spill some northern blood.

Goldie ignored him, keeping his eyes locked on Pat. The runner made hurried steps toward a minivan that was idling at the curb, waiting for him. He looked around nervously, but his eyes never turned in the direction of the car that was coasting toward him. Goldie tightened his grip on his hammer, anticipating closing the curtain on Pat's life. He was just positioning himself to deliver the kill shot from the window, when a second person emerging from the building Pat had just left gave him pause.

"Wait a minute, Daddy!" A little girl of about ten or eleven came running down the walkway toward Pat. She was a pretty little thing with chocolate skin and thick black hair she wore in two Afro-puffs. In her hand, she held a piece of construction paper that flapped in the breeze. "You forgot the picture I made you!"

"Thank you, Rose." Pat hugged her. Rose wasn't his biological child, but he had been raising her with her mother since she was four years old. Her father had walked out of their lives shortly after she was born, and only made random guest appearances.

"Fuck!" Goldie cursed and slunk back in his seat. He'd almost made a horrible mistake.

"What you doing, man? You had him in your sights!" Snake pointed out. He was clearly upset about Goldie not taking the shot.

"He's got his kid with him. We gotta do this another time," Goldie told him.

"Fuck that! Buda said he gotta die today, so he gonna die!" Snake barked. Before anyone could stop him, he had gotten out of the slow-moving car and was making his way toward Pat and Rose.

"What is this idiot doing?" Hank asked. He looked around nervously to see if anyone was hip to them and their intentions yet.

"I got him," Goldie said and got out to chase down Snake.

Pat was giving Rose a hug and telling her again how beautiful the picture was when he felt a presence behind him. He turned, a man he had never seen a day in his life walking up on him. He didn't know the man, but the gun in his hand told him what he wanted. Before the man could reach him, Pat took the knapsack off and dropped it at his feet. "I already know the routine, just take the bag and go. I don't want any trouble." He raised his hands in surrender and positioned himself between Snake and Rose.

Snake snatched the bag up and slung it over his shoulder. "Thanks," he told Pat, before shooting him in the head.

The sound of a gunshot and Rose's screams drew the attention of the driver of the minivan. He looked up in time to see Pat's body hitting the ground. He was supposed to be protecting the runner, but had been so preoccupied with his phone that he never saw the gunman creeping up. He jumped out of the van and tried to bring his Glock into play, but Goldie shut him down when he shot him twice in the chest.

When Goldie was sure that the driver was dead he turned his attention to the mess Snake had created. Rose was leaning over Pat's dead body, screaming for her daddy to wake up while Snake laughed menacingly. Goldie had always known Snake to be a piece of shit, but shooting a man in front of his child was a new low. Just when he thought he couldn't be any more disgusted, Snake raised his gun and pointed it at the child.

"What the fuck are you doing?" Goldie grabbed Snake by the arm.

"This little bitch has seen us. That mean she gotta go too," Snake said and jerked free of Goldie. He was determined to make sure there were no witnesses to what he had done. Snake was about to blast the child, when he felt the press of steel to the back of his head.

"On everything I love, if you hurt this child you'll be joining her in the afterlife." He cocked the hammer back with this thumb to punctuate his statement.

Snake weighed his chances and decided against it. "You got

it, boss man." He lowered his gun and stuck it back into his waistband. Slowly he began to back away.

Goldie kept his gun pointed at Snake until he was away from the girl and back in the car. When he looked down at Pat's corpse and his grieving daughter, his heart sank. He was supposed to be in charge of the hit squad, but had let the situation get out of control. Goldie was a killer and had committed some gruesome acts, which he made no apologies for, but gunning a man down in front of his kid was a line that even he wouldn't cross. What troubled him more was the way Rose was glaring at him. Her eyes were no longer those of a frightened little girl, but those of the monster Snake had unwittingly given birth to.

"I can't believe you left that lil bitch alive to identify us," Snake fumed. He had been ranting since they left the crime scene.

Goldie remained silent, staring out the window and trying his best to ignore him.

"Why don't you give it a rest," Hank suggested. Unlike Snake, he was familiar with Goldie's moods. The quiet was the calm before the storm.

"Fuck that shit, Hank. You know that ain't how we do things!" Snake continued. "No witnesses, no prison time. That's been understood since we was shorties running around the wards. I don't know, maybe y'all been away from New Orleans too long and all this big-city living has dulled your edges—"

"Snake," Hank said in a stern tone, but the young man kept talking.

"—or maybe this little nigga only tough when his big brother around."

Without warning Goldie turned and shot Snake in his big mouth.

"Goddamn it, Goldie!" Hank almost lost control of the car when the gun boomed in such closed quarters. With his free hand, he wiped away the blood and brain bits that had splashed on his face. He spared a glance at what was left of Snake's face in the rearview and shook his head. "Buda ain't gonna take too kindly to the fact that you killed one of his people."

Goldie sucked his teeth. "Fuck that dishonorable-ass nigga in the back and fuck Buda too. If Buda wanna buck behind this, he knows where to find me and I know where to find him."

CHAPTER TWO

"Babe, about how much longer do you think we're gonna be?" Trudy asked for the fifth time in nearly as many minutes. She was a pretty slim girl with big tits, a pretty face, but barely a speed bump's worth of ass and a shitty attitude.

Shadowing her were two husky bodyguards, who looked like they could think of a million other places they'd rather be.

"We'd have been done if you would help me pick something instead of complaining," Oscar snapped, continuing to sift through the rack of expensive dresses inside Nordstrom. He was an older man with a hard face and kind eyes. As usual he wore one of his custom suits, this one purple with green polka dots. Oscar considered himself a fashion icon and boasted an impressive wardrobe of custom-made pieces, but no matter how much bread he spent on the clothes he always ended looking crazy. That had become kind of his calling card. Despite his appearance Oscar was a certified whiz with numbers. He laundered money for criminals and businessmen alike, but his biggest client was a man whom they called Big Stone. He ran Harlem.

Trudy sucked her teeth. "What the fuck do I look like, help-ing you pick something out for the next bitch and I ain't got no bags in my hands?"

"Cut it out, Trudy. I keep telling you that the gift is for my friend's kid. It's her birthday," Oscar reminded her.

"A likely story," Trudy said with a roll of her eyes. "If that's the case, why don't you just get her an H&M gift card? All teen-age girls seem to dig that store," she said sarcastically.

Oscar looked at her as if the suggestion was laughable. "You don't insult the most powerful man in the city by simply getting his daughter a gift card. Now get your ass over here and help me, or jump in a cab so I can call a more useful bitch to do what you can't," he barked.

Fifteen minutes later, Oscar and Trudy were leaving the store and the two bodyguards were weighted down with bags. Trudy helped Oscar pick out a couple of nice dresses, some shoes that he thought were atrocious, and a handbag that had a price tag equal to a mortgage payment. Oscar felt robbed with no gun, but Trudy as-sured him that Pearl would love the gifts. Considering that Trudy and Pearl were nearly the same age, he took her at her word. Of course, Trudy made sure he dropped a few racks getting her some things too, but for what he would make her do in the bedroom later, Oscar could stand the hit. One of the bodyguards went to fetch the car, leaving the other to guard over Oscar and Trudy, who were standing in front of the store.

Trudy was bumping her gums about something Oscar didn't catch because he was too busy looking over his cache of purchases. He had blown way more than he had planned to when he walked in the store, but he looked at it as an insurance policy. Things had gotten tense on the streets of New York over the last few months. There was a mysterious group of wild-ass outlaws overthrowing organizations and gobbling up city blocks like locusts in a wheat field. No one knew too much about them other than they were good at creating headaches. More than a few of Oscar's old clients had closed up shop, leaving the few who were still operational as Oscar's only lifelines. It was in his best interest to keep his big spenders happy, which is why he reluctantly went all out for Big Stone's daughter in hopes that the crime boss would recognize it and keep Oscar in his favor.

Oscar whipped out his phone and was about to text his barber to see if he could get a walk-in appointment, when a familiar melody gave him pause. He strained his ears to make sure they weren't deceiving him, and grasped on to a single horn playing "Goin' up Yonder." His mother would always sing it to him as a child. The song was one of the few positive memories he had from that period in his life. His eyes swept the block for the source of the music and he found it a few feet away from the store entrance. A young girl sat perched on a milk crate, pouring her soul through a dinged-up brass horn while a generous few tossed coins or the occasional dollar into the shoe box at her feet. With her hair in two French braids and doe-like eyes she didn't appear to be older than her teens, but she played the horn like someone who had been around far longer. There was a pain in her music that was so deep Oscar felt obligated to drop a hundred-dollar bill into the shoe box.

The girl stopped when she noticed the denomination of the bill, snatched it up, and stuffed it into the pocket of her tight jeans.

"Bless your heart, mister." She looked at him with thankful eyes. "Me and my six little brothers and sisters will be able to eat for at least two weeks off this!" she said in a deep southern accent.

"You keep playing that horn the way you do and one day you're gonna be somebody great, kid," Oscar told her sincerely. Just then the bodyguard pulled to the curb in a big black SUV. The second bodyguard popped the back door open and held it for Oscar and Trudy. Oscar was leading Trudy to the vehicle when the girl stopped him.

"Boss man, you been so kind to me, I'd like to repay you if I can. Allow me to see you off with a song," the girl offered.

Trudy sucked her teeth. "You already gave this little tramp a hundred dollars and she still trying to squeeze you for more?"

"Oh no, this one is on me, ma'am. It's a pretty little tune that I think you especially will enjoy." The girl pursed the horn to her lips and began to play "Farewell, My Friend."

Oscar was so enthralled by the girl and her beautiful horn playing that he never noticed the beat-up white station wagon inching up and blocking their SUV. The bodyguard behind the wheel honked the horn in frustration, barking at the station wagon to move. In reply the back window rolled down and someone poked the barrel of a shotgun out of it.

All eyes turned to the sound of the shotgun being fired. Lead pellets smashed through the windshield and peppered the face of the bodyguard who had been behind the wheel. Time seemed to slow, as Oscar watched the bodyguard spill from the SUV, clutching his ruined face. From the wagon hopped two men wearing ski masks. The lead man was tall and slender, and moved with the grace and speed of a cat. He leapt atop the car and hit the first bodyguard twice more in the back, finishing him. The second was squat with shoulders as wide as a small sedan. Though a mask covered his face, it couldn't contain the thick beard poking out through the mouth hole. Still armed with the smoking shotgun, he lumbered toward Oscar.

"The devil come to collect his due." The bearded masked man sneered, cocking the slide of the shotgun.

The second bodyguard wouldn't be taken down so easily. He drew a big .357 and let it rock with abandon. One of the powerful shells hit the slender masked man, knocking him off the car and evening the odds. With him out of the way the bodyguard turned his attention to the one with the shotgun. He'd just got him in his sights when the girl who had been playing for them stepped into his line of fire. The bodyguard hesitated, which would cost him. With a twist, she yanked the mouthpiece of her brass horn free, and drove the stiletto hidden inside into the bodyguard's throat.

At the sight of the two dead men Trudy let out a high, shrill cry; until then Oscar had forgotten she was even there. She was clearly terrified, and seemed rooted to the spot with fear. Oscar had no such hang-ups. Leaving Trudy to whatever fate had in store for her, he bolted. He figured if he could make it back inside the crowded department store the killers would be less likely to gun him down.

As Oscar was trying to make his way back into the department store, someone was coming out. Oscar was moving so fast that he ran smack into the young man. When Oscar felt the Kevlar vest beneath his hoodie a chill ran down his spine. The lower half of the young man's face was covered by a red bandanna, but Oscar could see his eyes. They weren't the eyes of a killer; in fact they seemed almost remorseful over the tragedy that was about to befall Oscar. That didn't change what had to happen and they both knew it. With an empathetic nod, he ended it quickly for Oscar by putting a bullet in his heart. Oscar's body had barely hit the ground before his killer was out the department store doors.

It took everything Domo had to keep up his brisk pace and not break into a run. At least two dozen people had seen him shoot Oscar in the doorway. Though the bandanna covered his face, he couldn't help but feel like all the witnesses knew exactly who he was. It wasn't supposed to have gone like this. He was simply there as backup while Buda and Willie did the wet work, but once again he found himself thrust into the role of executioner. Since he had started running with the pirates it seemed to happen to him more often, and he was starting to care less. Just as Vita had promised, delivering death had started to feel like a part of the job and it troubled him.

When he made it outside he found that Buda had made a mess, as was his MO. Two men laid dead on the ground, and a girl with big fake tits was huddled in the corner screaming her head off. On the street Vita was helping Willie to his feet and into the car, where Lucky drummed his fingers on the wheel nervously. From the way Willie clutched at his chest it looked like he had taken one during the firefight. Everything had gone to shit and Domo was standing in the middle of the heaping pile.

"You take care of the old man?" Buda approached. The mask still covered his face, but his beard gave him away.

"He's laundered his last dollar," Domo assured him.

"Good kid." Buda slapped him on the back with his meaty

paw. "This crew might make a man of you yet. Dust this yelling bitch so we can get out of here."

"Wait . . . I haven't seen your faces and I swear I won't tell anyone." Trudy regained her composure enough to plead for her life.

"Yeah, but you know our names. Ain't that right, *Domo*?" Buda asked slyly.

Domo gave him a look. He knew what was happening. Buda was trying to back him into a corner and force his hand, but Domo wouldn't be bullied. "Fuck that. I murked Oscar, but I ain't killing no female."

For a few ticks the two men stood there glaring at each other. It was a test of wills. When it finally looked like Buda was going to back down, he surprised Domo by snatching his gun out of his hand. Before Domo could offer up any sort of protest, Buda shot Trudy in the forehead. He then turned the gun on Domo. "When I tell you to shoot a muthafucka, you better put a hole in them or I'm gonna put a hole in you. We clear?"

Domo's jaw tightened. "Crystal."

CHAPTER THREE

Asia stood wide-legged with one foot slightly in front of the other. She was finding her balance. Her arms were outstretched and locked at the elbows. She had practiced the positon many times, but each time felt like the first. She measured her breaths, in and out, until she found a rhythm. The Glock in her hand was heavier than the small nine-millimeter she was used to shooting with so she had to adjust her grip to compensate for the weight. She cleared her mind of everything except what she was aiming at and tapped the trigger.

"Much better," her boyfriend, Knowledge, said and stepped away from her; he had been watching her intently.

"I don't feel like I did anything different." Asia sat the gun on the table in front of her and removed the earmuffs.

"That's because it's becoming more natural to you." Knowledge hit the button to retrieve the paper target. "You see," he pointed at a hole that was an inch or two above where the heart would've been if the man was made of flesh instead of paper, "you're to get your whole body in sync with the gun instead of just your eyes. You're compensating for kick and trajectory so it's helping with your aim."

"But I still didn't hit the bull's-eye." Asia pouted.

"Because there's a part of you that's still fighting against it." Knowledge hooked in a fresh target and hit the button to send it back. He kept going until it was twice the distance from where Asia had been shooting. He picked up the gun and took aim. Knowledge drew in a breath and squeezed the trigger as he let it out. The gun boomed four times, flicking the target this way and that. When he pulled the target back there were four evenly spaced holes in the face of the paper man. "It's like a battle between what your body wants to do instinctively versus what you're being taught."

"You're always showing off." Asia nudged him playfully.

"I'm not showing off, just making sure my lady is armed with all the necessary skills to make it in life," Knowledge told her.

"I highly doubt I'll be firing up anything but a stove in culinary school." Asia laughed.

"My baby, the world-famous chef." Knowledge hugged her close to him.

"You're getting ahead of yourself. First I have to graduate and then I'll probably have to slave on someone's line in a restaurant for at least a year before I can even start thinking that far ahead," Asia told him.

"Not if I buy you your own restaurant."

"You've been saying that for years, Knowledge."

"That's because I mean it, boo. I've been putting in overtime stacking this bread up so we can bring that dream of yours to fruition. You've been holding me down for years, so it's only right that now I'm starting to get my weight up I return the favor," Knowledge said seriously.

"I have been with you since you were a nappy-headed little devil out in the streets causing all kinds of hell," Asia joked.

"Girl, you bugging. My head ain't never been nappy!" Knowledge declared, snatching off his Yankee fitted and running his hand over his waves.

"Hey, do you remember when we first met? You worked your ass off to get my phone number."

"Yup, to this day you're the first and only woman I've ever gone to jail for."

It had been roughly five years ago when Knowledge first met Asia. Back then he was still hustling corners for Big Stone, but was fast making his way up the criminal ladder. He had been on the block hustling all day with his friends without eating so they all decided to go to McDonald's. Asia was working there at the time as a cashier. From the moment he laid eyes on her, he knew he had to have her and so he pushed up.

Knowledge cut in front of five people on the line and ambled up to the counter, where Asia was taking someone's order. "What up, shorty? You know you way too fine to be in here flipping burgers," he capped.

Asia paused long enough to roll her eyes at him and reply, "And what should I be doing? Hanging out with your dusty ass smoking weed? You know you reek of it, don't you?" She went back to helping her customer.

Knowledge sniffed his shirt. "C'mon, I ain't mean it like that.

I just think you're fine and I was wondering if I can get your number or something."

"No," Asia said without looking up.

"Why not?"

"Because I don't know you." She handed the customer his order and waved the next one forward.

"Then you can get to know me. I ain't a bad dude, Ms. Asia," he read from her name tag.

"Look, I know you see me working so can you either get your thirsty ass back in line and place an order or leave?" Asia shooed him. He was cute, but she could tell by the way he talked and dressed that he was a street dude.

"Oh, so you like to play hard to get, huh? That's okay, I'm persistent," he said, obviously not taking the hint.

"Everything okay out there, Asia?" the manager called from the back, where he had been watching the exchange. He recognized Knowledge's face from seeing him around the neighborhood so he already knew what he was about.

"Yes, everything is fine," Asia told him. "Look," she lowered her voice, "you about to get me fired for holding this line up. Can you please go?"

"I'll leave once you give me your number."

"Look, you think you're the first guy to pop some slick shit thinking it's gonna make me get all gushy and give you my goodies? If you really want my number then impress me; set yourself aside from every other thirst bucket looking for a good time."

"You got that," he said with a smirk, backing away.

Asia thought that the young hustler had finally gotten the

memo and she was rid of him, but what she didn't know was that Knowledge was a young man who loved a good challenge. Each night thereafter he would show up and try again. The second night he came, he was carrying flowers; she shot him down. The third night he swapped out his hoodie for a button-up shirt and a box of candy; again she shot him down. Asia wouldn't admit it to him, but Knowledge was starting to wear her down with his persistence. It wasn't until the fourth night that Knowledge would finally make his way to her heart.

It was just before the end of her shift when she noticed him walk in. This time she was curious to see what he had come up with to try and get her to go out with him. He waited patiently on the line until it was his turn to order. "You just don't quit, do you? Okay, what kind of lame-ass trick do you have for me tonight?"

Knowledge shrugged. "The only one I got left." He climbed up on the counter and got down on one knee. "I've come in here every night and tried to offer you something that I know most girls go for, but what I've come to realize is that you ain't most girls. What I've come to you with tonight is plain old honesty. I'm feeling you, girl, and I wanna show you that I ain't a bad guy. So if I gotta embarrass myself to prove to you that my intentions are genuine then so be it. Asia, would you do me the honor of allowing me to take you on a proper date?"

It seemed as if every eye in McDonald's was on Asia, including her manager's. Asia was both shocked and embarrassed. She'd had guys try all sorts of tactics to get next to her, but none had ever gone quite as far as Knowledge.

"I'm calling the police," the manager threatened, grabbing the phone off the wall and dialing 911.

"Boy, are you crazy? You're gonna get yourself arrested!" Asia told him.

"And it'd be worth it if it brought me one step closer to making you mine," Knowledge said sincerely.

"Girl, say yes so this fool-ass boy can get down and I can order my food!" a woman called from the back of the line.

"You know how folks love McDonald's fries, baby. So what you gonna do?" Knowledge asked her playfully.

Before she could answer a pair of hands grabbed Knowledge by the back of his hoodie and snatched him off the countertop. The manager had made good on his threat and called the cops. They slammed Knowledge to the ground and slapped handcuffs on him. Even as they were dragging him out of McDonald's, he kept looking at Asia, waiting for an answer.

Knowledge was taken to the local precinct, where he spent the next couple of hours being processed. They eventually let him go with a desk appearance ticket for disturbing the peace. When he walked out of the precinct he was surprised to find Asia outside waiting for him. "That was the craziest shit I've ever seen." She pressed a slip of paper into his hand before walking away. Knowledge had finally gotten her phone number.

"They fired my ass right after the police took you away." Asia chuckled. "But looking back, it was worth it."

"So, what now? You wanna let off a few more rounds?" Knowledge asked.

"Nah, I've smelled enough gun smoke for the day. I am hungry, though."

"Bet, let's go grab a bite. What you feel like eating?"

"Take me to Red Lobster for lunch like you used to when you were a young broke nigga trying to impress me." She looped her arm in his and they started for the door.

"You gonna stop trying to play me." He laughed as they strolled through the parking lot.

"So, how does Pearl feel about me coming to her little party tonight?"

Knowledge shrugged. "No clue, I haven't told her yet."

Asia stopped short. "Are you freaking kidding me? How do you think Pearl is going to feel when she sees you walk in with a staff member from her school on your arm?" Asia was studying to be a chef, but it was the board of education that paid her bills. During the day she worked as a security officer at Pearl's school, which explained why Knowledge always seemed to know what Pearl was up to. Asia was his eyes and ears during school hours.

"Honestly, I don't care. The only reason I'm even going is out of respect for Big Stone," Knowledge said.

Asia was about to say something when Knowledge's cell phone rang. It was his trap phone, so Asia already knew it was a business call. "Speak," he answered the call. His face took on a dark expression as he listened. Whatever news he was receiving wasn't good.

"Everything okay?" she asked once he was off the phone.

"Nah, baby. I'm gonna have to take a rain check on lunch. I'll drop you off at the crib, then be back in time to pick you up for the party." He opened the passenger door for her. "You know Big Stone likes his bad news delivered in person."

CHAPTER FOUR

Pearl sat at the make-up counter at Rouge Salon, wearing a disinterested look as the cute older woman on the other side beat her brown face to a flawless glow. Elaine, who was the owner of the full-service salon, usually attended to Pearl personally whenever she came in, but Elaine was out for the day so Pearl had to settle for her stand-in, a slightly older woman whom she had never seen there before.

Sandra had initially turned her on to Rouge, which was right in her backyard, but Pearl had never given it a second look. Sandra and Elaine went back to their days on the fast track, so when Elaine finally got it into her mind to go legit and open the salon, Sandra did what she could to help steer business her way. It was a relatively new shop but was becoming very popular. Pearl had been skeptical at first, but after she saw how Elaine and her girls had laced her it became *her* spot from there on.

She raised her hand to run through her hair, as she often did when she was stressing about something, then remembered that she'd had it cut a few days prior. Her friends had been shocked when they saw the new look and her father almost blew a gasket, but Pearl didn't care. It was her hair, and she wanted a change. Absently, she scrolled up and down through her phone's call log, briefly pausing every time she came across a number that she hadn't used in over a week. Part of her was tempted to hit *call* but her pride wouldn't allow it. Pearl didn't chase men, even ones she thought she loved.

"A guy or money?" The woman behind the counter snapped her out of her daze.

"Excuse me?" Pearl wasn't sure what she meant.

"You've got a look in your eyes like something is weighing heavy on you, so I figure it's either a guy or money," the woman explained.

"Who are you, my therapist?" Pearl asked defensively.

"I didn't mean nothing by it, honey. You just look like you needed a compassionate ear. No disrespect."

"You worry about my face and let me deal with my personal life," Pearl suggested with a roll of her eyes.

"Could you be any more of a bitch?" Marissa cut in. She was seated at the next table with a younger girl working on her face. Marissa was a gorgeous dime of Cuban descent. Her skin was dark and smooth with cocoa undertones. Her thick black hair was braided into tight knots, which she would let out right before the party and let her curls hang.

"What you mean?" Pearl asked as if she had no clue what she was talking about.

"I mean you sitting there looking like somebody kicked your dog, then getting all snippy when she asked you about it." Marissa rolled her neck. "You've had that puppy-dog-ass expression that's been plastered across you face for the last few hours, and that sour-ass mood is starting to spill over, so you might wanna get it in check."

"My fault, Marissa. I guess I've just got a lot on my mind," Pearl admitted.

"The only thing that should be on your mind is your birthday party tonight. This shit has been the talk of school and the streets," Marissa reminded her.

"Belated birthday party," Pearl corrected her. Pearl's birthday had come and gone nearly a week prior, but without the fanfare she had been hoping for. She'd had a small dinner celebration with her family and a few friends, but there was to be no party . . . at least not then. Something was going on in the streets that had her father nervous and he put the whole family on lockdown. It was only after they attended the funeral of one of Pearl's best friends that her father finally relented and agreed to the party in an attempt to pick her spirits up.

"Better late than never," Marissa said.

"You're right, and I'm trying to get as excited as everyone else about it but . . ." Pearl's words trailed off. "I don't know, it just doesn't feel the same without the whole crew being there."

Marissa's mood darkened a bit. "Yeah, I can't front. It ain't gonna be the same without Sheila there with us."

Sheila had been a member of their little quartet and one of Pearl's closest friends. A week prior she had convinced Pearl and Marissa to sneak out to a party some older guys she knew were throwing at a bar in Harlem that belonged to a local gangster they called Pops' Brown, who Pearl would find out later was an asso-ciate of her father's. Pearl wanted to leave early, but Sheila and

Marissa insisted on keeping the party going with the guys. Before Pearl left she and Sheila had gotten into a nasty argument and said some cruel things to each other. The next day Pearl would get the horrifying news that Marissa was in the hospital and Sheila was dead. A freak fire had broken out in the bar. Marissa was lucky enough to make it out with minor injuries, but Sheila had gotten trapped inside with some of the other partygoers when the building went up. Thinking about the things she had said to Sheila and would never be able to take back made Pearl want to cry, but she had spent too much money getting her makeup done to ruin it and didn't have time to start the process over again.

Pearl let out a sigh. "I wish I had just made both you guys leave when I did. Then maybe Sheila would be with us tonight."

Marissa motioned for the makeup girl to pause the brushing of her lips and turned to Pearl. "Mami, you should know better than that. If you had to try and force either of us to leave it'd have only made us want to stay more. There's nothing you could've done about what happened that night, Pearl. Let it go."

Marissa was right, but it didn't stop Pearl's mind from toiling over a series of what-ifs. The party definitely wouldn't be the same without Sheila, but there was the absence of another that also weighed on her.

As a girl Pearl had enjoyed reading stories about love at first sight and white knights who swooped in to make honest women of damsels, but to her they were little more than entertainment. Her father had seen to that. Big Stone didn't raise his kids to look at life through rose-colored lenses; he allowed them to see the world for just what it was. There were no happy endings for little ghetto children unless they went out and wrote them themselves.

That's exactly what Pearl thought she was doing when Diamonds walked into her life, writing her own happy ending. This was not to be. Diamonds was gone, and so were his empty promises. His parting gift to her was a jewel that she would carry close to her from then on: Be careful how freely you give your heart.

"You ladies about ready to go?" Power's voice drew Pearl from her thoughts. He'd been in the same spot for the last hour while the girls got their makeup done, sitting on a wooden chair guarding their dozen or so shopping bags. Power was a pale young man with a stocky build, and ocean-blue eyes. With his golden-blond hair, which he always rocked in cornrows, Power could've easily passed for white, but he was actually biracial, inheriting most of his father's features, but hardly any of his mother's.

"Chill out, P. It takes time for a lady to get her face flawlessly beat. We shouldn't be too much longer, though," Pearl assured him.

"Cool. I don't mean to rush you, but I promised Knowledge and your dad that I'd have y'all back to the house by a decent hour," Power explained.

"Right, just doing your job." Pearl rolled her eyes and turned back to let the woman finish her makeup. From the corner of her eye she could see Marissa giving Power a hungry look. "Don't even think about it," she whispered, reading her friend's mind.

"What?" Marissa asked innocently.

"Don't *what* me like I don't know what you're thinking, slut!" Pearl teased her.

"C'mon, don't act like the thought of jumping his bones has never crossed your mind!" Marissa accused. "That blond hair and tight-ass body." She fanned herself. "I don't usually go for white dudes, but he can get it."

"Power isn't white. He's black and Puerto Rican," Pearl informed her.

"Get the fuck out of here!" Marissa looked from Power to Pearl disbelievingly. "Papi," she called to him, *"te gusta este tono de lápiz labial?"*

Power pondered it. "The red lipstick looks good on you, but I think a darker shade would play better on your skin."

Both of the girls burst out laughing, leaving Power with a dumbfounded expression on his face, trying to figure out what the joke was.

"So I meant to ask you earlier, what's with all the extra security today? I don't mind having Power's fine ass hanging around, but I spotted some unfamiliar faces in front of your place when I came to meet you this morning. Is everything cool?" Marissa quizzed.

"Girl, just some hood shit." Pearl waved her off as if it were nothing. "I overheard Knowledge telling my dad the other day that some big-time dealer they knew got killed. So my dad being the paranoid person he is felt like we needed added security until things cooled off."

"Is that why you got a bodyguard? Are we in danger?" Marissa asked nervously. She had known Pearl's family for years, and the Stones put the *G* in "gangster." She could remember times when she was little, how Pearl's dad, Big Stone, would creep to their house late at night to pick up her father, Tito. Every time Tito came back from one of Big Stone's midnight rides it would take him days to get over whatever they would see or do on those trips.

"Oh nah, we're civilians and the real niggas respect that," Pearl assured her. "Power is with us because I finally told Knowledge about Devonte."

"That nut-ass nigga who was stalking you?" Marissa gasped. Their other friend Ruby had told her the story about the older guy Pearl had been sleeping with who didn't know when to back off.

"Yeah, do you know he had the nerve to pop up at my house one night?" Pearl shivered thinking about the night Diamonds dropped her off on her block and Devonte had been there waiting for her.

"Ruby told me! Mami, I would've been scared shitless," Marissa admitted.

"Shit, I was. If it hadn't been for Stoney there's no telling what might've happened to me that night," Pearl said seriously. Stoney was her little brother. He stumbled upon them as Devonte was trying to force Pearl into his car and backed him off with a gun.

"Yo, I can't even picture Stoney holding." Marissa laughed. She knew him as the thin, basketball-playing kid who loved to try and feel her butt.

"Neither could I until I saw him shooting at Devonte's ass. I think I was more afraid of him going to jail for murder than I was of Devonte dying," Pearl said. "I could never forgive myself if my brother threw his life away over some hood rat shit I started."

"I feel you, Pearl, but we both know that shit is in your blood. Y'all are Stones. Stoney is a good kid, but he's at that age where he could go either way. Keep your good eye on him, Pearl."

Pearl didn't know how she felt about Marissa's delivery, but she couldn't argue with her assessment. She and Stoney were third generation in a family that had been breaking the laws of New

York state for nearly a century. They attracted a certain element and it attracted them.

"Anyhow," Pearl changed the subject, "after what happened, Knowledge insisted that I have somebody shadow me when I'm too far from home. He didn't trust any of the other guys to do it so he called in Power."

Marissa cut her eyes at Power. "He must be as dangerous as he is handsome if Knowledge trusts him enough to guard the princess."

"I haven't known him that long, but word on the street is that back in the days he was a real beast out here. Him and Knowledge came up together, but Power got out of the life after he came home from prison. He's a square now, just doing a favor for his friend."

Marissa shook her head. "I can't even get one dude of Knowledge's caliber to look my way, and here you got two of them that's willing to lay down and die for you. You're a lucky girl."

Pearl shrugged. "If luck is what you wanna call it. People on the outside looking in always think shit is sweet because we got cars, money, and power, but all this comes with a price, even for those of us who ain't in that life. You have no idea what it's like to live in the Kingdom of Stone."

A half hour later the girls were all made-up and ready to go. The woman who had done Pearl's face had laced her. She looked radiant by the time she raised up from the chair. Pearl felt so bad about how she had spoken to her that she gave the woman a fifty-dollar tip and a sincere apology. "I'm sorry for the way I snapped at you earlier," she said and slid the bill across the table.

"It's okay, sugah. I was your age once and I can still remember my first heartbreak."

"And what makes you think it was my first?" Pearl asked curiously.

"Because the pain is still fresh on your face. After you've had it happen to you a time or three, each one will hurt less and less."

"So how did you get over your first heartbreak?" Pearl asked.

"That's a complicated question with an even more complicated answer. My first true love was an older man who was originally from Trinidad, but had been living and hustling in New York for a few years. By the time I met him I had already had a kid from a previously failed relationship, but he didn't seem to mind it. Him and my son got along pretty good, probably because he was always buying him things." She laughed. "My man was real free-hearted with money because he was sure getting plenty of it. He was a drug dealer, but trying to go legitimate. He had this idea to create his own slice of Las Vegas on the East Coast by building a casino in Newark. I think his vision was what I loved about him more than that sexy-ass body and them long dreadlocks. He was the first man I ever met, including my daddy, who ever encouraged me to dream. When I was with him I believed that anything was possible because he told me it was."

"Damn, sounds like he had some powerful game," Pearl said.

"Yeah, he had game, but it was more his presence than anything. Tom was a man who when he entered a room you felt him long before you saw him. Now I ain't no fool; when you meet a man who was handling like mine was, it's expected for him to have women on the side. It bothered me some, as it should've, but I accepted it because I was queen. It was all like a dream to me, and I got my wake-up call when I told him that I was pregnant."

"Wasn't he happy?" Pearl asked.

"Happy enough to tear my heart out and stomp on it. Turns out that I wasn't his queen, his wife was."

"Wife?" Pearl clasped her hand over her mouth in shock.

"Yup, a wife and three kids that I didn't know anything about. I was so love-struck that I even offered to play second place just to hold on to a piece of the lifestyle he had given me. He told me that having it get out that he had gotten one of his mistresses pregnant wouldn't look good to the men he was trying to get into business with. I was getting rid of the baby willingly or forcefully, but my bastard wouldn't stain his good name. After that he shoved a bag of money into my hands and had one of his flunkies escort me to the abortion clinic."

"Did you get the abortion?" Pearl asked. The minute the question left her lips she realized how insensitive it must have sounded. "Sorry."

"No need to be," the woman assured her. "I came close. I didn't wanna get rid of my baby, but sitting in the car with that killer, I didn't reason I had a choice. Then God stepped in. The man Tom had sent to take me to the abortion clinic pulled over and told me to get out. I don't know what caused him to defy his boss and let me go, but I didn't question it. I did as he ordered and got my ass out. With the hush money Tom had given me, I packed up my son and disappeared to New Jersey. A few months later I had my second son."

"What a piece of shit he was for trying to force you to kill your baby!" Pearl fumed.

"I've called him that and much worse over the years. Eventually I was able to get over my hate for the man who had crushed my soul. I let that grudge go and left it to God to sort out. The point of me holding you hostage and telling you my story is so that maybe it'll help you with what you're going through. The ones who claim to love us the most are the ones who hurt us the worse. The weak bitches curl up and die behind it, but those of us who are strong always bounce back. I was able to get over my Thomas, so you'll be able to get over whatever loser has done you wrong too."

Pearl smiled. "I needed to hear that . . . thank you. Listen, you really hooked me up today so I'm gonna ask for you again the next time I come in here."

"Thanks, but this was a one-shot deal for me. I'm friends with the owner, Elaine, and she asked if I could help out because they're short-handed today. I just came in to make some quick cash," the woman informed her. "But I do freelance work, makeup and hair. For the right price, I even make home visits." The woman took a business card from her pocket and handed it to Pearl. "My name is Carla. Just give me a call whenever you're ready."

Pearl tapped the card against her fingers before slipping it into her purse. "I'll do just that. Take care, Carla." She turned to leave but stopped short. "If you don't mind me asking, did you ever see him again? Your first love?"

The woman's face darkened. "Yes, once after that day. He made the five o'clock news when he was gunned down coming out of a restaurant in Manhattan. They say it was over drugs, but I like to think it was his karma catching up with him."

"Damn, what were y'all doing, swapping life stories?" Marissa asked sarcastically when Pearl finally re-joined her.

"Shut up, hussy. I was apologizing for making an ass of myself earlier and getting her information. She got skills and she makes house calls." Pearl pulled out the card and showed it to her.

Marissa snatched the card and looked at it. "Oh, she got a nine-seven-three number." She frowned and handed Pearl the card back. "She one of them Jersey bitches . . . probably from Newark."

"I wouldn't care if she was from the moon, Carla got skills!" Pearl declared.

"That she does." Marissa admired Pearl's makeup. She glanced back and the direction they had just come and watched Carla, watching them. "Yo, why do I feel like I've seen her before?"

"Let's hope you didn't sleep with her husband or no crazy shit," Pearl joked. "Come on so we can get back uptown and change clothes. I can't be late to my own party."

Power brought up the rear, weighed down by their bags, while Pearl and Marissa walked a few feet ahead gossiping. Marissa was just giving Pearl the dirt on the orderly she had met during her short stay at the hospital and how she was thinking about sleeping with him when she saw Pearl's eyes lock in on something just ahead of them. She turned to see what her friend was looking at and all she could do was roll her eyes. "This nigga here."

CHAPTER FIVE

By the time the police arrived on the scene to clean up the mess outside the department store, the pirates were long gone. They had abandoned the station wagon in a parking garage a few blocks away and hopped in an SUV, which also held a spare set of clothes for each of them. It confused Domo how Buda was worried about powder residue, but not getting caught with the dirty guns he'd opted to keep. Those rested in a pillowcase that sat between his legs on the passenger-side floor. Buda had a thing about not tossing away guns that were still in good working condition. He had some people who would break them down and use the parts for other guns to commit more murders. Buda was a strange man whom Domo had been trying, to no avail, to figure out. He must've felt Domo's eyes on him, because he looked back and flashed a sly smile in his direction. Domo wouldn't forget the fact that Buda had drawn a gun on him, and neither would Buda. They'd definitely have a discussion about it at a later time.

Lucky sat behind the wheel of the SUV, steering with both hands, trying his best not to crash. He pretended he wasn't nervous, but Domo could smell fear coming from his pores. Lucky talked as much shit as the rest of them, but Domo knew he wasn't built for the kind of games Buda had them playing.

One-eye Willie was in his own world, examining the bruise on his chest. The vest had stopped the slug, but Domo could tell from the way he winced every time he touched the bruise that it hurt like hell. He'd got the name One-eye Willie because of the glass eye shoved into the left socket of his skull. It was as black as onyx with a gold pentagram painted where the pupil should be. There were several stories about how he had lost his eye, but the one most whispered about was that Willie had removed the eye himself. They say he was born with a veil, the ability to see spirits. As a kid the ghosts plagued him so bad that he took a fork and tried to pop his eyes out so he wouldn't see them anymore. The only thing that saved his other eye was his grandmother catching him in the act. Willie was a whack job, but he and Domo got along okay.

Lucky and One-eye Willie were two of the dozen or so new faces Buda had brought to New York. When he had assumed control of Diamonds' crew, the first thing he did was start bringing in some of their affiliates from other cities they had left their stains on. Hank and Goldie had been opposed to the move, but Buda fed them a line about needing to beef up their numbers after what had happened to Diamonds. Soldiers from Florida, Texas, and even New Orleans had answered Buda's call to arms for the last week and been running amuck in New York.

"You good?" Vita asked, snapping Domo out of his train of thought.

"I'm straight. Still a little pumped after the job, ya know?" Domo lied.

"How's that tender-dick nigga's nuts ever gonna drop if you keep babying him, Vita? Let me find out you showing this nigga more than the ropes," Buda said in an accusatory tone.

"Fuck you, Buda!" Vita gave him the finger.

"*Fucking* might be the root of our little problem here." Buda's eyes swept between Domo and Vita like he knew their secret. There were whispers about the true nature of their relationship, but no one had been able to confirm it as of yet. Buda had been waiting for years to try his hand with Vita, but Diamonds had always been in the way. As far as he was concerned she was now fair game and he wouldn't lose his shot to an outsider.

"What's the matter, Buda? You ain't getting none at home so you making up fantasies in your head?" Domo interjected. He had meant it as a joke to take them off the subject, but the dead silence that fell over the SUV told him it hadn't been taken that way. It wasn't the first time Domo had mouthed off to Buda, but it was the first time he had done it in front of the new faces.

"You know," Buda turned his entire body around in the seat and leveled the full weight of his gaze on Domo, "you been on some real funny shit lately." In his hand dangled one of the pistols that hadn't made it into the bag.

"Buda—" Vita began, but was cut off by a sharp look.

"I got a joke I can tell too," Buda returned his attention to Domo, "but this one ends up with us having to get the whole back of this vehicle hosed out. Like to hear it?"

Domo's mouth suddenly became very dry. He didn't think Buda would shoot him in the back of the SUV, but with a man like him you could never really tell what he was capable of. He knew he had to choose his next words carefully. "That sounds like a joke that would leave us short a member. If we short a member, then maybe next time the runaway mark finds freedom through those department-store doors instead of death."

Buda glared at Domo for what felt like an eternity, before letting his thick lips part into a smile. "You ain't as dumb as you pretend to be, kid." He turned back around in his seat. Buda had been trying not to like Domo, but he had to admit that the young man was growing on him. He was a cool character who would pop his gun and had proven to be dedicated to their cause. If the time ever came when Buda found the need to get rid of Goldie, Domo would prove a more than capable successor. The only problem with bringing Domo in fully was that his greatest asset was also a potential liability: his loyalty. It had been Diamonds who accepted Domo into the crew, so how would Domo feel if Buda's part in Diamonds' disappearance ever came out?

"You are one crazy little fucker! The last dude who talked slick to Buda went missing the next day." One-eye Willie laughed.

"Don't gas him up, Willie. The night is still young," Buda warned. "And why are you even talking shit when you almost got laid to rest back there? What would make your fool ass jump on top of the car like that?"

Willie shrugged. "I saw Hannibal do it one time on an episode of *The A-Team*. Shit been on my bucket list for years!"

The whole car erupted into laughter.

"Yo, I'll bet that old-ass nigga ain't gonna feel so big after he finds out two major pieces just got knocked off his chessboard!" Lucky attempted to add a joke of his own to the merriment. For this he got a sneaky jab to his side from Buda.

Domo saw it, but acted as if he didn't. "Drop me off on the corner," he told Lucky.

"I'm not stopping until we get to the Bronx," Lucky told him. He wanted to get the dirty guns out of the car and away from him as quickly as possible.

"Cool out with all that nervous shit and just let me out, homie," Domo reiterated. This time his tone was sharper.

Lucky looked over at Buda, who gave him an approving nod. "Fuck it," he muttered and reluctantly pulled over on the corner near the train station on 110th Street.

Vita gave Domo a questioning look, to which he replied by patting her thigh reassuringly before climbing out of the car. Much to everyone's surprise, Buda got out too. two and a half sets of eyes watched intently as the two men stood toe to toe on the sidewalk.

"What's up?" Buda asked.

"Ain't nothing. Gotta few moves I need to make," Domo told him.

"I know you ain't salty about me drawing on you back there, is you?" Buda asked suspiciously.

"Nah, man, that's a conversation for another time," Domo said coolly. "I gotta go see somebody real quick, if you know what I mean?"

Buda looked over his shoulder at Vita, who was ear-hustling through the cracked rear window. "You young boys are always so quick to put pussy over money!" he said loud enough for Vita to hear. "Fuck it, handle your business. We gonna go to the spot and get this money straightened out. You gonna come by when you're done handling your business?"

"I'll scoop it tomorrow," Domo said, which surprised Buda.

"How do you know it'll still be there?" Buda asked suspiciously.

"You might be a lot of things, Buda, but you don't strike me as a man who leaves debts unsettled."

Buda laughed. "You're right about that. Make sure you come see me in the morning. I hold on to your money too long and I might be tempted to trick it off," he half joked. "Oh, and there's something else. Goldie caught a lick for some powder while we were taking care of the old man downtown. We're still working through what we got from Eddie's people a few days ago, so I was thinking we hit you and L.A. with the powder we ripped off today to see what you can do with it. That's if you think you can handle it?"

Domo thought on it. "I'd have to check and see what we got left from the last package you dropped on us. Since we're just starting out, things are still moving kind of slow."

"So you saying you boys ain't equip to handle volume?"

"I never said that, I just said I'd have to do a tally of inventory. Don't wanna take more product from you when we still ain't finished paying you for the last batch. I don't like debts."

"I can dig that, shorty. Tell you what; how about I drop the coke on you anyhow. You boys kick me up the bread for half the shipment when you can, and the other half you can consider as a gift. Something to help you guys get on your feet over that way."

"So, you just gonna give us free coke out of the goodness of your heart?" Domo was suspicious.

Buda laughed. "You should know by now that I ain't got no heart. But to answer your question, it's a reward for your services.

You been a loyal solider to this crew, Domo. And the coke is my way of saying I appreciate it." He extended his hand.

"Thanks." Domo shook Buda's hand.

"Cool, I'll have one of my people drop it off to you and L.A. either tonight or tomorrow. Unless you want me to hold on to it and you can take it yourself when you come back to pick up your money?" Buda asked slyly.

"Man, you know I ain't throwing no stones at the penitentiary. We'll be waiting for your delivery." Domo turned to head for the train station.

"Yo, Domo!" Buda called after him. "How far are you willing to go to be rich?"

"Buda, if you still gotta ask that question then you obviously ain't been paying attention."

"Everything good with the youngster?" Willie asked once Buda was back in the vehicle.

Buda played it off. "Yeah, everything straight. You know these lil niggas be in their feelings. That boy better learn to man up if he plans to make the cut with this crew."

"If you ask me, I think he'll do more than make the cut," Willie said, watching Domo as he went down the train station steps.

"And how the fuck do you know that and you just met him?" Buda asked.

Willie pointed to the glass pentagram in his eye. "Because I can see it in him. If you're smart, you'll keep that boy close."

CHAPTER SIX

Domo didn't have to stop at the tollbooth to pay his fare, because he made a habit of keeping a metro card on him at all times. He hadn't found himself on public transportation much lately, but old habits died hard. He made it to the platform just in time to catch the southbound number 2 train. Domo hated New York public transportation and had thought about taking a cab downtown, but it would be too easy to follow and Domo didn't want anyone clocking his movements. Traveling underground would make it easier for him to disappear in the shuffle.

The measure was paranoid, but it wasn't as if Domo didn't have reason to be. From the time Domo had met him, Buda had never made it a secret that he was opposed to Diamonds letting Domo and L.A. into their crew, but Vita had spoken for them and so had their own actions. Domo and L.A. had proven themselves in everyone else's eyes, but Buda still didn't seem convinced that the kids from Newark were built like that. This is why when Diamonds went missing and Buda assumed control of the crew, Domo expected to be bounced out on his ass, but instead Buda promoted him. He set Domo and L.A. up with some product and some guns and gave them his blessing to open up shop on the other side of the Hudson. Buda wanted to expand, and claimed the gesture was a test to see if they could stand on their own. But to Domo it felt like it was done more to keep them at arm's length from whatever he had going on in New York. Domo didn't venture into New York much anymore unless it was to put in work, which there had been no shortage of.

Things were heating up in the Apple. During Diamonds' conquest of New York he had run afoul of some cats who supposedly put him in the ground. Buda refused to sit idle with his best friend dead and someone trying to stop them from getting money, so he declared war, but who were they fighting? He kept Domo and L.A. on a need-to-know basis, claiming he still wasn't sure how far he could trust them. Even Vita hadn't been able to offer Domo a straight answer, only telling him that Buda would let them in eventually and so long as he remained loyal, the crew would always take care of him. Her words seemed sincere enough, but he also knew that there was something she wasn't telling him and that didn't sit right. L.A. might've been cool with busting his gun blindly so long as they got rich in the process, and it made Domo feel good to be able to finally help his mother, but Buda would have to do more than throw money at him if he expected Domo to remain a part of their crew. He needed answers, sooner rather than later.

He exited the train on 135th Street and started walking south. His mom was working at one of her side jobs, at a salon in Harlem.

Since Domo happened to be in New York too and had a few dollars in his pocket, he wanted to surprise her by treating her to a bite to eat.

Domo's mom was the backbone of their family and hands-down the strongest person he had ever met. She came from what he came from, the streets, and both her sons' fathers had walked out on her, but that only made her go harder. Domo's mom worked two and sometimes three jobs to make sure he and his older brother, Understanding, always had clothes on their backs, a roof over their heads, and food in their bellies. They had endured some tough times and sometimes she had to go without so that they could eat, but she did it without once complaining. She did what she could to make sure her boys wouldn't suffer through life's pitfalls, but the ghetto had a way of snatching children when their parents weren't looking. When Understanding went to prison, Domo's mom doubled her efforts to provide for Domo, determined not to let the streets or the system take both her boys, but there was only so long a young man could sit by and watch his mom struggle, so Domo did what he had to do to ease his mother's burdens.

Just as Domo was going in through one set of doors of the salon, some familiar faces were coming out the other. He almost didn't recognize Pearl since she had cut her hair, but she was still as fine and curvaceous as ever. She was the older sister of his friend Stoney, and the muse for some very explicit dreams that Domo had had. He'd always had the biggest crush on the slightly older girl, but would never admit it or act on it, out of respect for his friend. Besides, Domo was hardly Pearl's speed. She was into men who had paper and power, much like her father. She hadn't noticed him yet, so he was just going to slide into Macy's and act like he hadn't seen her, but her friend Marissa killed that plan when she capped, "This nigga here."

"Oh hey, what's up, y'all? I didn't even see you," Domo lied. When he moved to greet Pearl the white boy stepped between them.

"Hold on, kid." Power laid one of his thick hands on Domo's chest.

"It's cool, P. That's one of Stoney's little friends," Pearl told him.

When Pearl used the word *little* to describe Domo it hurt, but he didn't show it. "What y'all doing so far from the Kingdom of Stone?" he asked sarcastically.

"We had to come get our faces right for our girl's party." Marissa preened, showing off her makeup.

"Damn, you having a party and I didn't get an invitation?" Domo looked at Pearl, faking hurt.

"Negative, it's eighteen and older and you ain't eighteen yet," Marissa answered for her.

"Neither are you!" Domo shot back.

"Y'all two knock it off." Pearl was tired of Marissa and Domo's bickering. They went through it every time they saw each other. "Domo, I don't want you to take this the wrong way because you're a cool little dude, but this party ain't your speed."

"What does that mean?" he asked.

"It means there's going to be a certain caliber of guys at my party—boss niggas—and you ain't even a solider in nobody's army. I wouldn't want you to feel out of place," Pearl said honestly. She hadn't meant to offend him, but she had.

This time the hurt in Domo's eyes was real. "Damn, it's like that?" He'd always thought Pearl to be a cool chick, but now he wasn't so sure.

"Domo, you know what I mean." Pearl tried to clean it up. "Besides, you're one of my baby brother's friends. How would it look on me to be partying with you?"

Domo took a step back as if she had shoved him. His pride was wounded, but he did his best not to show it. "I hear that hot shit, Pearl." He turned to walk away, but had a parting thought to share. "You know what? You're absolutely right, Pearl. I ain't a soldier in nobody's army, because I got boss in my blood and can't never see myself waiting on another muthafucka to feed me. I'm gonna go out and get it, because that's how my mama raised me. One day you're going to remember this conversation, bet that." He stormed off.

"Don't you think you were kind of hard on him?" Power asked once Domo was out of earshot.

"Please, I ain't stunting that little wannabe gang-banger and his feelings. He'll get over it," Pearl said dismissively.

"I know that's right!" Marissa gave her a high five.

Power smirked. "Y'all think y'all got it all figured out, huh? I'll tell you like this: the same cats you meet on the way up are the same ones you meet on the way down."

When Domo pushed open the door of the salon, it was with a little more force than he intended, which got him a dirty stare from the girl sitting at the appointment counter. He gave her an apologetic look and kept stepping. When he had first asked Pearl about his invite to the party he had only been joking, but her reaction had made it personal. Pearl always gave Domo grief about being a young street dude, but she had never outright tried to play him before that day. The only reason he didn't disrespect her was because she was still Stoney's sister and Big Stone's daughter. The last thing he wanted was a late-night visit from Knowledge over some words. Still, the things she'd said to him resonated. He was tired of people looking at him as little Domonique. In due time, they would all see that he had as much potential to be great as anyone else. Pearl didn't know it, but she had just lit the fuse to a powder keg.

He took his time strolling passed the different booths and eye-balling the ladies working them. Rouge definitely had some eye candy working its stations. He found his mother behind a counter with her back to him, while she packed away the tools of her trade. The younger girl who worked the counter with her spotted Domo and started to say hello, but he motioned for her to be quiet. He eased up on his mother and whispered softly, "Excuse me, love. I was wondering if you'd do me the honor of joining me for lunch?"

Carla spun, lips pursed to dismiss whoever was pressing her, but her face softened when she spotted her baby boy. "Domonique, you play too much." She swatted at him affectionately. "What you doing here, boy?"

"I was just coming from a job interview in the neighborhood and wanted to see if I can grab a bite with my old lady right quick."

Carla looked at her watch and then at what he was wearing. "A job interview in the middle of the day? Dressed like that?" She rolled her eyes. "Boy, you know your mama ain't no square, so come correct."

Domo thought about insisting his story about the interview were true, but his mother had always had an uncanny ability to see through his bullshit. "A'ight," he began, "this older guy I know needed me to watch his back while he pulled some BS in a department store." It was the truth, but not in its entirety.

Carla grabbed Domo by the arm and pulled him out of earshot of the young girl, who was trying to act like she wasn't eavesdropping. "Domonique, what do I keep telling you about throwing stones at the penitentiary!"

"Ma, I told you I was only the lookout. I was in and out of the store in less than two minutes."

"That's even worse! If you're simple ass had gotten caught you'd have done just as much time as the one who actually committed the crime, so you might as well have gone all the way with it!" Carla barked. She saw the look that flashed across Domo's face and checked herself. "Look, I didn't mean it like it sounded. You know I'd never encourage you to break the law. It's just been a long morning; I'm tired and just in my feelings a bit."

"Everything okay?" He noticed the troubled look on her face.

"Yeah, just dwelling on people, places, and things that no longer hold any weight in my life," Carla said. Her conversation with Pearl had stirred old memories and old feelings. "But don't try and change the subject. I'm serious about what I said, Domonique. I don't want you out here playing in them streets. I know you're a young man now and will have to figure out certain things on your own, but that doesn't stop me from praying every night that you can hold on to your innocence as long as possible. This game can make killers out of good men and I couldn't see that happen to my baby."

His mother's words rang with truth, and were appreciated if also too late. She knew her baby boy dabbled, but Carla really had no idea how far down the rabbit hole he'd plunged and he didn't have the heart to feed her another lie so he just nodded. "So, you gonna let me take you to eat, or what?"

"I wish I could, baby, but I gotta get to my other job," Carla told him, while finishing packing her supplies.

"Damn, Mama. All you do is work," Domo said in frustration.

"Watch your mouth," she scolded. "And if I didn't work, who gonna keep the lights on?"

"I told you I'm down to help," Domo reminded her.

"And you will, right after you finish high school and get a good job. For now, you handle the books and I'll handle the bills." She popped the handle of her roll-on bag. "I gotta hustle so I can make it to my next gig. Call to let me know when you get in the house." She kissed his cheek and rushed off.

PART

THE HOUSE OF
THE RISING SUN

CHAPTER SEVEN

Knowledge stood in the corner of the basement, leaning against one of the tall arcade games. His eyes followed the big man as he stormed back and forth, breaking whatever was in arm's reach. In all the years he had worked for him he couldn't ever recall seeing him quite this angry. As Knowledge observed the rant he could feel his heart beating in his chest, not out of fear, but anticipation. He knew what would come next. It was the only option they had left, but he still wasn't sure if it was the right one.

"I can't believe this shit!" Big Stone said in his husky voice, finally taking a pause from his path of destruction of his furniture. "That's two more of my top people gone in the last twenty-four hours. These niggas must think I'm some kinda fucking sucker, huh? I'm gonna show them what it is, though, when I rain fire down on their bitch asses!"

Knowledge had just come back from Jersey and delivered the bad news he'd received from one of his informants. Another one of Big Stone's packages had been hijacked. That made the third in the last week. He was upset about it, but that wasn't what had

sent him through the roof: his top money launderer had been as-
sassinated. Oscar had laundered thousands for Big Stone on a
monthly basis and now he was gone. One thing you didn't fuck
with was Big Stone's money, and he had made tons of it over the
years with Oscar.

"Stone, please try and calm down, man. We need to assess the
situation before we rush into it," Black cautioned. He was an older
dude who had history with Big Stone that went back to the days
when they were selling nickel bags of weed at parties. In his day
Black had been notorious for his skills with a pistol, but getting
shot six times forced him to come in off the streets and join upper
management. In addition to being Big Stone's voice of reason,
Black also ran pussy out of several cathouses he and Big Stone
owned around the city.

"That's easy for you to say, Black. Ain't nobody in the streets
pissing on your name, are they?" Big Stone barked. "That's the
problem. I been too calm about this shit instead of in the streets
taking heads, but it's a new day! I want everybody in this crew
that's able to hold a gun in them streets fucking shit up."

"But we don't even know who we're fighting," Knowledge
said. The minute he opened his mouth he regretted it.

"And whose fault is that?" Big Stone turned angry eyes to
Knowledge. "You're supposed to be my eyes and ears on the streets,
but lately you don't see or hear shit. Was I wrong by putting you
in positon as my number two?"

"Of course not, but—"

"But shit!" Big Stone cut him off. "Somebody is taking out
bosses all over the city, but don't nobody seem to know nothing.

It's like we're under siege by damn ghosts! What's it gonna take for me to finally get some results, me ending up like Pana?"

Pana had been the first domino to fall. He was a Spanish cat who commanded a small army of killers out of Washington Heights that had a reputation for brutality. People had been trying to knock Pana out of the box for years and all attempts had failed until recently. A group of unknown assailants had swept in and eradicated Pana and his entire crew in under twenty-four hours. Pana's death sent a clear message to everybody hustling in the streets of New York: no one was safe.

"You know I'd never let that happen," Knowledge told him.

"I don't know shit except that you're sitting on your damn hands while I'm losing money, resources, and respect. At least a dozen of our people have either been killed or abandoned ship since this shit started. I can't say that I blame them, from the way we've been running things lately. Who wants to work for a boss that they feel like can't protect them?" Big Stone asked.

"We did turn up something from Oscar's murder, though I don't know how helpful it is," Knowledge offered.

"Well, don't keep an asshole in suspense. Spill it, nigga," Big Stone ordered.

"In addition to the four guys in the mask there was also a female with them."

Big Stone gave Knowledge a look. "How is that helpful? You know how many niggas employ women in their crews these days?"

"But how many that play a brass horn?" Knowledge shot back. "One of the witnesses said that Oscar stopped to listen to a street performer playing a horn, which is how they got the drop on him."

Big Stone smiled. "That's the Knowledge I know. Now we got something to go on. Any ideas of who she might be running with?"

Knowledge rubbed his chin in thought. "Well, there's Christian Knight. I know he has a girl working in his crew, and I hear he and his group have been moonlighting as contract killers, but this ain't really his style. He's more of a pill pusher and a pimp."

"What about them other broads from down the way? What do they call themselves, Twenty-Gang or something?" Black asked.

"Nah, ain't been too much going on with them since Eve disappeared," Knowledge said.

"Now that broad was a piece of work!" Big Stone recalled. "Knowledge, I need you to get out in the streets and shake some trees. We need to get out ahead of this thing ASAP."

"You got it, OG," Knowledge assured him before heading back up the basement stairs.

"That boy has come a long way from when you first brought him in," Black said.

"Indeed he has. I knew he was going to be special long before he did and that's why I kept him so close all these years."

Knowledge first came to Big Stone's attention at the ripe age of twelve, and even back then he had been moving way faster than most kids his age. His father was a ghost and his mother was a smoker so most times he was left to his own devices. You could always find him in the streets committing petty crimes like shoplifting from supermarkets and boosting from stores, but then he got his hands on his first pistol and stepped his game up, dabbling in armed robbery. He had gotten away with taking off several neighborhood dealers, but his luck ran out when he got it in his mind to rip off one of Big Stone's spots. When the gangster's crew finally tracked Knowledge down and brought him before Big Stone to answer for what he'd done, Big Stone's initial thoughts were to kill him and string his ass up as an example to anyone else who might've thought about trying it, but when he looked into the young man's defiant eyes he saw something: himself. Having also had a rough upbringing Big Stone understood how desperation could sometimes push a man into making unwise decisions. So instead of giving Knowledge death, he gave him an opportunity.

Those closest to Big Stone thought it would send the wrong message to the streets, giving the kid who had stolen from him a job, but Big Stone never cared much about public opinion. He started Knowledge off small, slinging stones on corners, to see how far he could trust him. It wasn't long before Knowledge proved himself to be not only a good earner, but a loyal soldier, and Big Stone never had to tell him to do something more than once. A year after coming to him Knowledge had gone from slinging on corners to giving out packages. He was a natural leader, and the corner boys followed him without question. After a while Big Stone began to realize that Knowledge's talents were being wasted on the streets, so he brought him in out of the cold. Nearly a decade later, Big Stone knew that letting Knowledge live had proven to be one of the best decisions he had ever made.

"You okay?" Black asked Big Stone, noticing the far-off look in his eyes.

"Yeah, I'm cool. I just got a lot of shit on my mind," Big Stone told him. "We been playing this game for a long time, Black, and I ain't never encountered no shit like this. How the hell am I supposed to fight an enemy I can't identify?"

"Don't fret over it, Stone. This ain't the first time we've had our backs against the wall and we're gonna come out on top like we always do. Regardless of how this plays out, you know I'm with you until the end, like I always been," Black assured him.

"Well, shit, don't put us in the ground just yet." Big Stone laughed.

"Speaking of things needing to be put in the ground, one of my little birds whispered a piece of new in my ear that I think you might find interesting. Your baby mama is back in town."

"Zonnie? You have got to be shitting me!"

"I wish I was. I hear she's been crawling in and out of dives around town trying to recruit girls for her escort service. She tried to press a few of mine and the only reason I didn't have her put down was out of respect for you."

"Hell, I wish you would've. It'd have saved me the trouble of doing it. I should've taken that bitch's life instead of just her keys when I kicked her foul ass outta my place!" Stone went back to his pacing. "First my slimeball brother crawls out from whatever rock he is hiding under and then my low-down baby mama slinks back into town. This is a bad omen, Black . . . a bad omen."

"I've had some of our people out trying to get a location on Rolling, but so far nothing," Black told him.

"Yeah, he's always been good at moving like a ghost. Just ask his kids," Big Stone joked. It was common knowledge that Rolling Stone had fathered at least six kids and wasn't in any of their lives. "Well, keep looking. I wanna know what that piece of shit is doing back in New York after I banished his ass."

"What should we do if we find him? You want he should disappear again, this time permanently?" Black asked. He had never liked Stone's brother and made no secret of it. Rolling had always

been jealous of Big Stone, even to the point of once trying to or-
chestrate an attempt on his life. Black had foiled the attempt, which
was how he had ended up taking the six bullets.

"Nah, man. For as much of a snake as he is, he's the only sib-
ling I got left living. Besides, I promised my mama on her death-
bed that my parents would never have to bury any more of their
children. So as long as my daddy is still alive, so is Rolling."

"Speaking of your dad, how is Bo?" Black asked.

"Still as mean as a bear that been woke up early out of hiber-
nation. I swear that man ain't got a lick of love for nobody outside
his grandkids," Big Stone said.

"Sounds like the Bo I remember. See, you a little younger, but
I had the pleasure of knowing your daddy when he was in the streets
heavy. Man, I tell you, that nigga was the definition of a soldier."

Bo Stone was a gangster with a résumé that stretched back to
the fifties. He had been one of the few old-timers who had been
opposed to selling drugs, instead making his money through stick-
ups, girls, and a host of other illegal activities. He'd predicted what
drugs would do to black communities and wanted no part of them.
When the Italians started trying to flood Harlem with heroin, Bo
Stone had been one of the few to stand up to them. When they
sent their people at him he would always send them back in bags.
He was a one-man killing machine and eventually everybody got
the message that no drugs would be sold in his neighborhoods.
The people he protected praised him as if he were a black super-
hero. It was such an ironic twist of fate that his son Big Stone had
grown up to be one of the biggest dealers in Harlem.

"Yeah, my daddy was a soldier, and now he's just a pain in my
ass. He's supposed to be coming to Pearl's party tonight."

"That's great!" Black said excitedly. Growing up, Bo had been one of his heroes.

"Speak for yourself. I got enough that needs handling tonight without having to hear a bunch of bullshit about how I'm bringing down the black community. These muthafuckas was getting high before me, and they'll continue to get high long after I'm gone."

"Whatever you say, boss. And what you wanna do about your baby mama?"

"Rolling is off limits, but that bitch fair game if she steps wrong. The last thing I need is her popping up and fucking with my boy's head. I don't want that bitch Zonnie nowhere near my son! You hear me, Black?"

"How could I not when your ass is screaming like a crazy person?"

"I'm sorry, man. I just got a lot going on in my head right now." Big Stone took a seat on the couch. "On another note, did you confirm everybody for tonight?"

"Yeah, and most of them agreed to come."

"What the hell do you mean, *most*?" Big Stone gave him a questioning look.

"Man, after what happened to Pana and then Pops, most have gone underground and ain't trying to stick their heads out until this shit blows over."

"Bunch of pussies, all of them!" Big Stone said heatedly. "For as much money as I done put in them niggas' pockets, I gotta twist their damn arms to take a meeting with me now? Well, fuck 'em! We gonna come out of this on top and when we do, I'm not gonna forget the ones who turned their backs in times of trouble."

"Does Pearl know what's going on?" Black asked.

"In all the years you've known me, have I ever involved Pearl in any of this street shit?"

"I know it, Big Stone. I'm just thinking she may get suspicious when all them gangsters start showing up at her thing tonight," Black explained.

"Nah, man. She'll just think they're coming out to pay respect for her birthday. Ain't no need to spoil it by telling my baby girl that her party is cover for a war council."

CHAPTER EIGHT

When Knowledge opened the basement door he felt it bump into something. Peering around it, he found a woman rubbing her forehead. This was Sandra; she kept the house in order and helped Big Stone with the kids. She was nearly as old as Big Stone, but it was hard to tell because outside of the gray running through her thick black hair, the years had been kind to her. She had bright brown eyes that seemed to twinkle when you looked into them, and a body that had held together quite well over the decades.

"Oh, hey, Knowledge," Sandra greeted him, trying her best not to look guilty.

"What you doing huddled behind the door looking all sneaky?" Knowledge asked playfully, as if he didn't already know the answer. She had probably been ear-hustling in on everything that was going on downstairs. There wasn't too much that went on under the Stone roof that she didn't know about.

"Just doing a little straightening up," Sandra lied, fake-dusting the plant rack near the door. "Everything okay down there? I thought I heard something break?"

"Big Stone just having one of his moments."

"Well, I hope he don't expect me to come down there and clean up behind his ass. Ain't no more babies in this house. You wait until he gets his ass up here and I'm gonna get him told!" Sandra declared in her sassy drawl.

"Probably best you leave it alone for right now," Knowledge warned her.

Sandra had been around Knowledge long enough to be able to read his moods. Something was troubling him. "I've noticed he's been in a pissy mood lately. Anything I should be concerned about?"

"You know I'd tell you if there were. This is just some street shit. I'm on it, though."

"Well, you know it becomes more than that, I ain't afraid to bust my gun to protect these kids," Sandra said seriously.

"You can take the dog out of the fight, but not the fight outta the dog." Knowledge laughed.

Despite her kindly appearance, Sandra was a gangster. Back when she was still in the streets she had been one of Big Stone's most trusted runners, even having gone to prison twice. Once was for killing her abusive husband, and the second time had been for transporting drugs for Big Stone in and out of Maryland. She'd faced heavy time, but even under that kind of pressure Sandra never once opened her mouth. She took her time on the chin and when she was released, Big Stone was right there waiting for her, as he always was; but this time instead of offering her a package, he had a legitimate job for her. Pearl's mother had already passed by then and Big Stone was struggling to raise his daughter on his own. He brought her on as a governess to help him maintain the home and help him to raise his little ones. She was one of the few people he would trust to look after his children as well as his stash.

Sandra shook her head. "You know with as much money as that fool has got squirreled away, you'd think he'd sit his ass down somewhere and enjoy old age. You've proven that you're more than capable of handling things, and I've even told him as much."

"You know how Big Stone is. He does everything in his own time. I'm about to do some quick running around before I go home and get ready for tonight."

"You do that and make sure you're on time, Knowledge. I'm anxious to finally meet this young lady you been hiding." Sandra smiled.

"I haven't been hiding her, Sandra. You know I just like to keep my business and personal life separate."

"Save that for them shifty dudes you run with on the streets. We family, boy. You best not forget that," Sandra told him.

"Yes, ma'am." He kissed her cheek. "Let me go bust this move. I'll see y'all in a few hours."

Passing through the living room Knowledge came across the young prince of the family, sitting on the couch playing video games. Stoney and Pearl had the same father but different mothers, and Stoney had inherited most of his mother's features, from his fair skin to his pink pouty lips, but had gotten his height from his father. At sixteen years old he was already six-two and growing more every day. He was a straight-A student and a killer on the basketball court, but also a magnet for mischief, so Knowledge made it a point to always check up on him.

"Sup, lil man," Knowledge greeted him.

"Sup," Stoney replied, never taking his eyes off the big-screen television. His thumbs flicked feverishly across the controller.

"What you doing playing video games out here instead of in your room?" Knowledge asked.

"It's a way better gaming experience playing 'Call of Duty' on a sixty-inch TV versus a forty-two inch," Stoney explained.

"Well, pause that shit for a minute, I wanna holla at you."

"Okay, in a minute," Stoney said, continuing with his game. He was in a heavy firefight and needed to concentrate. The next thing he knew the screen went black. Stoney looked up to find Knowledge holding the power cord in his hand. "Damn, why you do that?"

"Because when I speak I expect you to listen, not put me on hold while you playing some damn game," Knowledge shot back.

Stoney threw his hands up in frustration. "Okay, Knowledge. You got it. What's up?"

"They let you back in school yet?" Knowledge asked. A week before Stoney had been suspended for fighting with a kid over a debt. He was running a football pool and a sore loser tried to beat Stoney out of what he owed, so Stoney beat him. In addition to his father's height he had also inherited his father's violent temper.

"Yeah, it was only a three-day suspension. I'm good now. And before you even ask, yes, I shut down all my rackets," Stoney told him.

"Good man." Knowledge nodded. "You make sure you keep your ass out of trouble and your mind on them grades. There's a lot of colleges looking at you and if they start thinking you're one of those headache kids it could hurt your chances of having your pick of them."

Stoney sucked his teeth. "You bugging! Any college that passes on me is stupid, because I'm the coldest point guard in the city."

"Confidence is good, but don't get so caught up in your own hype that you think this shit can't go to the left. You know how many dudes I know that are better than half the jokers in the league, but they fucked up their shots to prove it because they couldn't keep their noses out of the streets? You got all the physical skills to be good, but it's the ones who also have the discipline that go on to be great. Feel me?"

"Yeah, man. And you're right," Stoney said, more wanting him to leave so he could get back to his game than agreeing with him.

"What's up with them cats from Jersey you always be with? I don't see them around too much anymore." Knowledge was referring to Raheem and Domo. They were two knuckleheads from Newark whom Stoney knew from playing in the summer leagues. At one point they had been regular fixtures in the house, but had been noticeably absent lately.

Stoney shrugged. "I been too focused on school and practice to really hang out like that lately. I spoke to Rah the other day, but I ain't heard from Domo in a minute."

"Really, why not?" Knowledge asked, curious. Of all Stoney's friends Domo was the only one he liked. He was a quiet young dude who didn't say much but watched everything.

"Between me and you, I think he's back in the streets. The only time me and Domo go this long without speaking is when he's up to no good. He knows I gotta keep a clean reputation, so he avoids me when he's doing dirt."

This surprised Knowledge. Generally, kids Domo's age didn't take those kinds of things into consideration, and it was moves like those that made Knowledge respect Domo. He was young, but moved like he was an old-school gangster. He saw great potential in Domo, which was why he had approached Big Stone about bringing him in. Knowledge wanted to groom Domo, as had been done for him, but Big Stone shot the idea down. He didn't want any of Stoney's friends that close to the business. Still, Knowledge held on to the hope that Big Stone would one day change his mind rather than run the risk of losing out on a promising young soldier. Little did Knowledge know they were already a dollar short and a day late.

"Well, if you happen to hear from him, tell the young boy to holla at me." Knowledge tossed Stoney the power cord back.

As he was about to go out the front door, Pearl was coming in. Knowledge had to do a double take when he saw her. With her face made up and her hair freshly done she looked much older than eighteen. She was chatting away with her friend Marissa, while his friend Power brought up the rear, struggling with the bags they had forced him to carry. When Pearl noticed Knowledge standing there, she gave him the once-over.

"Why am I not surprised to see you here?" Pearl asked sarcastically.

"Shut up with your big-ass head. You think you all that because you got your little shit laced." Knowledge reached out like he was going to touch her hair.

"Stop playing." She giggled and ducked out of his reach.

"Hi, Knowledge." Marissa batted her eyes at him.

"Sup." He went back to his serious demeanor. Marissa was a hot-in-the-pants chick who was always trying to play him close, so he threw up a wall between them.

"Peace, God." Power lumbered into the house and sat the bags down so he could give Knowledge dap.

"Maintaining." Knowledge hugged his friend. "How was the babysitting expedition?"

"More trouble than it was worth. These chicks can do some shopping!" Power declared.

"It's hard work staying this fly." Pearl fluffed her hair. "Where's my dad?" she asked Knowledge.

"In the basement, but give him a little space for a few. He's been having a rough day."

"Good looking out on the heads up. That means I'll be in my room until it's time to leave. You still coming tonight, right?" Pearl asked.

"Yeah, I'll be there," Knowledge told her.

"He's bringing his girlfriend too," Stoney offered from the couch. He saw Knowledge give him a questioning look. "I overheard you talking to Sandra."

"I didn't know you had a girl," Pearl said. She knew Knowledge had chicks in the streets he dealt with, but this was the first she'd ever heard about him having someone serious in his life.

"Wasn't for you to know."

"Well, the bitch must be special if you're bringing her to my party," Pearl said, a bit more hostile than she intended to. She had been crushing on Knowledge since she was a little girl and was slightly jealous.

"She ain't no bitch, so watch your mouth. And she's special enough, which is all you need to know, so make sure you show the proper respect," Knowledge warned her.

"Whatever." Pearl rolled her eyes. "Come on, Marissa. Let's

go up to my room and start laying our outfits out." She led her friend across the living room and up the stairs.

"If she thinks she's salty now, wait until she finds out who it is," Power whispered.

"Shut up and come on." Knowledge pulled his friend out the door. "What you about to do?" he asked once they were outside.

"Since I'm off the clock, I ain't got shit to do. What's up?"

"Need to take care of a few things for Big Stone. Feel like taking a ride?"

CHAPTER NINE

Pearl had only begun to climb the stairs with Marissa when her little brother started in.

"Damn, ma. You looking good as hell today," Stoney told Marissa, undressing her with his eyes.

"I look good every day," Marissa capped.

"So," he eased up and draped his arm around her, "when you gonna take me out or something?"

"Take me out?" Marissa gave him a comical look. "Boy, you still get allowance from your daddy. Ain't nothing you can do for me or with me."

"Yeah, my daddy kicks me a little paper from time to time, but I get my own money too."

"Doing what?" Pearl cut in.

"Chill, Pearl. Why you gotta get all up in my mix?" Stoney asked with an attitude. Pearl was blowing his rap.

"You ain't got no mix, lil nigga." Pearl shoved his hand off Marissa. "And I know you better not be in school gambling again.

Knowledge might have let you slide with that bullshit, but if I catch you dirty, I'm telling Daddy myself."

"Whatever with yo snitching ass," Stoney mumbled and turned to go back to his video game.

"Oh, I saw your boy Domo a little while ago," Pearl told him.

"Word?" Stoney's eyes lit up. "Where you seen him at?"

"He was going in Rouge when we were coming out."

Stoney's face darkened. "Damn, he was right in Harlem and didn't even hit me?"

"Maybe he had something to do other than burn the day away playing video games," Pearl said. "And besides, maybe it's best you ain't hanging with him so much. I got a feeling Domo is into some shit you ain't ready for."

Stoney sucked his teeth. "You say that about all my friends."

"No, only the ones who run around with blood on their shoes," Pearl said, recalling the red specks she had seen on Domo's sneakers.

"So, y'all about to get all dressed up for your party?" Stoney changed the subject.

"In a little while, but not just yet. Only lames and ugly bitches get dressed hours before stepping out."

"Then you better get a head start." Stoney burst out laughing.

"Fuck you." Pearl flipped him the bird. "C'mon, Marissa. Let's go up to my room before I have to slap this slick-mouth little bastard."

"Wait a second, Pearl. I need to ask you something." Stoney stopped Pearl on her way to the stairs. The fact that he had paused his video game told her that it was serious.

"What's up, little bro?"

"You hear anything about my Zonnie being in town?"

The question caught Pearl totally off guard. Zonnie was the woman who had given birth to Stoney, but to call her his mother would've been a stretch. Big Stone had hooked up with her during a period of his life when he was trying to recapture his youth. She was young, and as fine as she was larcenous. They were together for a while, but Big Stone eventually got tired of her bullshit and kicked her out of his life. A year later she popped back up, but only long enough to drop a baby off on his doorstep. That was the last time Pearl had laid eyes on Zonnie until a week earlier, at the party she and her friends had been at. Zonnie was running girls now. Pearl hadn't told anyone, especially Stoney, about her run-in, so she wondered what made him ask about Zonnie after all this time.

"No, I haven't seen or heard from your mother in years," Pearl lied. "Why do you ask?"

"When Daddy was downstairs throwing his temper tantrum, I overheard him mention her name."

"Last I heard your mom was living on the West Coast and to my knowledge she's still out there," Pearl continued her lie. "Why, you thinking about reaching out?"

"Hell no! That bitch left me for dead, so she's dead to me," Stoney spat.

"Watch your mouth, that's still your mother!" Pearl scolded him.

Stoney sucked his teeth. "Sandra is the only mother I know or ever wanna know." He turned and went back to his game.

Pearl's heart went out to her little brother. Sandra filled a huge void in the house, but she wasn't their biological mother. At least

Pearl had got to know her own mother before she died, but Stoney had been so young when Zonnie dumped him off on Big Stone, Pearl doubted he even remembered what she looked like. Pearl and Zonnie had exchanged words over the subject when she'd bumped into her at the bar. Zonnie had accepted responsibility for ditching Stoney, but claimed the reason that she had never returned to his life was because Big Stone had forbidden it. Pearl knew her father could be a hard-ass, but couldn't see him preventing Zonnie from being in Stoney's life if she really chose to. That would've been downright cruel, and her father wasn't a cruel man, at least not that she knew of.

Leaving her little brother to his video game, Pearl and Marissa moved toward the stairs to her bedroom. As they passed the kitchen, Pearl caught a whiff of something tasty. Sandra was likely in the kitchen working her magic. This caused them to make a detour. When they reached the kitchen, Pearl found that her nose hadn't steered her wrong.

She found Sandra standing near the stove and watching her favorite show, *Law & Order,* on the small television mounted over the refrigerator. Sandra had been around for as long as she could remember, stepping up when Pearl's mother had died. She was their guardian and live-in housekeeper, but more important, she was the person Pearl could always turn to in times of trouble. She loved Sandra, not because she was the closest thing to a mother any of them had ever had, but because she never tried to take the place of Pearl's biological mother. She was more like an auntie or big sister than anything. Of course, Sandra wouldn't hesitate to lay down the law when the situation called for it, but she talked *to* Pearl instead of *at* her, like her father did.

"Something sure smells good," Pearl announced her presence.

"Hey, girls." Sandra wiped her hands on her apron. "I didn't realize you were back already." She kissed Pearl on the cheek, then Marissa. "How was shopping?"

Marissa chuckled. "Tedious, to say the least. Trying to keep up with Pearl in a store is like running a marathon."

"She learned from the best." Sandra smiled proudly. "I'll bet after all that shopping you girls are hungry, huh? I ain't whipping up nothing but a little stewed chicken and some rice, but you are more than welcome."

"You must be crazy if you think I'm going to eat this close to showtime and risk being bloated in my dress," Pearl protested.

"Speak for yourself. I'm starving." Marissa slid onto one of the stools at the breakfast counter.

"So, are you excited about your big night?" Sandra asked over her shoulder, scooping chicken into a bowl.

"Yup, just as ready to celebrate my birthday as I was last week when the party was actually supposed to take place," Pearl said sarcastically.

"You need to try at least pretending to be grateful, Pearl." Sandra sat a bowl down in front of Marissa. "Instead of having it late, you could've not had a party at all."

"I don't mean it like that, Sandra."

"Sure sounded like you did. Your father has got a lot on his plate these days and it'd be nice if you kids didn't add to it with those privileged attitudes you've been carrying around lately," Sandra said sternly. "You kids have no idea what your daddy is dealing with. There are forces at work beyond any of our control."

Sandra was obviously troubled about something, and Pearl responded, "What's with all the tension in this house lately? Is there something going on that I should know about?"

"Nothing for you to fret over, child," Sandra told her.

"Well, the streets have been talking lately and . . ." Pearl's words trailed off when Sandra shot her a look. Sandra had a strict rule about talking family business in front of outsiders. Pearl and Marissa had been friends for years, but Marissa wasn't a part of that side of their lives.

"You just do as your daddy says, when he says, and you'll be fine."

Big Stone appeared in the kitchen as if he could sense they were talking about him. "I thought I heard little birds chirping in here," he joked. "How's my baby girl?" He kissed Pearl on the forehead.

"I'm fine, Daddy. How was your day?" Pearl asked.

Big Stone shrugged his broad shoulders. "I've had better and I've had worse. How's it going, Marissa?" He turned his attention to Pearl's friend.

"I'm fine, Mr. Stone. Excited about tonight," Marissa told him.

"As you should be. This is going to be quite an event. I got people from all over popping through," Big Stone told them.

"Daddy, I hope you didn't invite a bunch of your old-school-ass friends. You know them dirty old men give me the creeps," Pearl joked.

"Only some of the most important men in the city. We're celebrating my baby girl seeing another year, so it's only right that they come to pay homage."

"That means it's gonna be some ballers in the house! Heeeyyyy!" Marissa did a little dance in her seat, which got her a whack from Sandra's dishcloth.

"You know we don't play that fast business in this house. You might not be one of mine, but I'll kick your tail like you was," Sandra scolded.

"Ouch, I was just playing." Marissa rubbed the spot on her thigh where the wet cloth had struck.

"Better not let Tito hear you playing like that," Big Stone warned. Marissa's father was one of his closest friends and a business associate.

"Mr. Stone, my dad is too caught up with board meetings to worry about what I'm doing," Marissa said. Unlike Pearl's father, who was heavily involved in her life, Marissa's parents were too caught up with work to spend any real time with her.

"Well, I'm concerned. When you're in my presence you get the same treatment as my kids, same as when Pearl is over at your place. Do you understand, young lady?"

"Yes, Mr. Stone," Marissa replied.

"Good, now you girls go on upstairs. I need to talk to Sandra," Big Stone told them.

"But she's eating, and you know how you feel about us eating in our bedrooms," Pearl pointed out. She just wanted to be nosy and try and catch a hint of what the adults were going to talk about.

"Well, since I'm the one that makes the rules, I can break them when I see fit. Now get, before I change my mind about this party. And don't let me catch you listening at the door either," Big Stone said. He knew Pearl's game.

"Okay." Pearl sighed. "C'mon, Marissa. Let's go try on our dresses."

"I swear, that girl is always trying to get over on somebody," Big Stone said once the girls had left the kitchen.

"I wonder where she gets it from?" Sandra gave him a knowing look.

"Shit, she don't get it from me. My cards are always on the table," Big Stone said.

"If that's the case, when do you plan on telling me what's been eating at you lately?"

"Girl, what you talking about? Everything is fine with me."

"That's bullshit and you know it, Lenox." Sandra called him by his government name. "You can bullshit them kids, but you can't bullshit me."

"It's nothing, just some street shit," Big Stone said as if it were no big deal.

"And that's the first thing that falls out of your and that fool Knowledge's mouth when you're trying to hide something. Come on with the real, or do I have to cut it out of you?" She grabbed a kitchen knife from the cutting board.

"Okay, just watch it with that damn poker!" Big Stone took a cautionary step back. He doubted she would really cut him, but with Sandra it was best not to take unnecessary chances.

"Okay, now spill it," she demanded.

"Things are getting a little tense on the streets."

"When are they not? I keep telling you that this is a young man's game, yet your old ass refuses to get up from the table. What is it now, some young upstart trying to buck for his piece of the pie?" she asked.

"More like a swarm of locusts trying to eat the whole pie. There have been a lot of bodies getting dropped on the streets over the last couple of weeks, and I ain't talking about no random soldiers getting clipped in the line of duty, I mean as in whole crews getting wiped entirely off the map. You remember what happened to Pops's spot, right?" Pops had barely made it out of his bar before the flames consumed it.

"Yeah, some type of electrical fire or something." She recalled what she'd been told about how the bar got burned down.

"Wasn't no electrical fire. Somebody torched the place," Big Stone revealed. "It took some prodding, but Pops finally told us what really happened. Somebody was trying to muscle him out of his bar, and when he wouldn't budge they burned him out."

"Oh my God," Sandra covered his mouth. "Did he have any idea who it was?"

"When me and Knowledge was visiting with him, he was about to give us a name before he mysteriously choked on his tongue. A day after that they found his son's body, or at least what was left of it. Police been searching for an entire week and still haven't found his head."

"Jesus." Sandra crossed herself. "Sounds like some dark shit at work."

"I think the people who burned Pops's bar were the same ones who took Pana out. Rolled right into the heart of his territory and cut his heart out of his chest in front of at least a dozen witnesses." Big Stone thought back on the horrible way Pana had been taken out. "Somebody is making their rounds and taking out some of the most respected men in the city."

Sandra picked up on his line of thinking. "And you think they may be coming for you next?"

"I wasn't sure at first, until Knowledge brought me word that Oscar and Pat bought the farm today too. Poor Pat, they killed him right in front of his baby girl."

"Oh my God," Sandra clasped her hand over her mouth, "that poor little Rose." She thought of the little girl Pat was helping to raise. "Stone, if this don't convince you to get out, nothing will."

"If I step away now, it'll look like I'm scared and every vulture in the city will be trying to get their taste of what I built."

"So, you're gonna let what people think of you put you in harm's way?"

"This is street business, you wouldn't understand."

"The hell I wouldn't." Sandra scoffed. "How many years was I out there putting in work before I came to work for you at the house? I been in the streets long enough to be able to retire from them because I got a nose for disaster and a knack for getting the hell out of its way. From what you've told me so far two things are very clear about these new players: Knowing how heavy Pana rolls yet they were still able to get to him means they are highly skilled. And the fact that they killed Pat in front of his little girl means that they have no moral code. God forbid if these men were to ever find their way to our doorstep, there would be no reasoning with them."

"Well, it ain't gonna get that far," Big Stone assured her. "I've got Knowledge and the rest of the boys out there turning over every rock and looking down every hole. We won't rest until we find these muthafuckas. In the meantime, I need you to do something for me."

"Anything, baby. You know all you've got to do is name it."

"In the event that anything should happen to me, I need you to look out for my kids," Big Stone said seriously.

"Quit with that kinda talk. Ain't nothing going to happen to you, and God forbid that it did, you know I'm gonna look after these children. Ain't I been doing it religiously for almost two decades?"

"For sure. I don't know what I would have done if it hadn't been for you stepping up. You been my backbone, and I know you always will be, but that wouldn't stand up in a court of law. Nah, we need to do this the right way."

"I know you ain't thinking what I think you're thinking?" Sandra asked hopefully. She had been sharing Big Stone's bed for roughly twenty years, even through up-and-down relationships. She wasn't happy with being a fifty-year-old side chick, but she had accepted the position with the hopes that he would one day come around, realize her worth, and make an honest woman of her.

"Hell nah," Big Stone said, realizing what she was hinting at. "Sandra, you know I love you, but I ain't trying to fix something that ain't broken. What I meant was making you the legal guardian of Pearl and Stoney on paper."

"Lenox—" she began.

"Just hear me out," Big Stone cut her off. "Outside of my daddy, I ain't got no family that I care too much about. You done already been in their lives almost as long as they been alive, and done a hell of a better job than they real mamas could've in making sure they turned out good kids. Who better to guide them into adulthood? You already on my life insurance, so why not on this?"

"Your life insurance?" This came as a shock to Sandra.

"Why do you seem so surprised?" he asked.

"I don't know, I just thought Pearl and Stoney would've been the logical choices."

"You know my kids being straight were my first priority; they got them trusts that I set up. The only one in this house who isn't financially protected is you, which is why I made you the sole ben-eficiary of my policy," Big Stone explained. "The policy ain't but for one-point-five, but that should be enough to keep your head over water while you sort everything out."

"I don't know what to say." Sandra was still in shock.

"Don't say anything. Just have your ass up Monday so you can go with me to the lawyer's office to make everything official."

"Thank you, Lenox," Sandra said, trying to keep her emo-tions in check. She had been taking care of people all her life and this was the first time anyone, including her ex-husband and her kids, had ever bothered to make sure she was taken care of.

"You know, me throwing around all this goodwill has worked up an appetite," Big Stone said.

"I just made some stewed chicken. You want me to fix you a plate?" Sandra picked up the ladle from the counter.

Big Stone pressed himself against her and plucked the ladle from her hand. "What I'm looking to eat ain't gonna fit on no plate." He planted soft kisses on her throat.

"You so nasty, cut it out." Sandra giggled as he undid her pants. "Them kids could come in here and catch us."

"Stoney is focused on that video game and Pearl is upstairs trying on clothes. We got at least a half hour before either of them comes this way. Now hush that mouth of yours and let me work mine." He pushed her pants down around her hips and got on his knees.

CHAPTER TEN

Pearl stood in the full-length mirror on the wall of her bedroom turning her body this way and that, trying to see if she liked the dress she was trying on. It was a fitted green number that would show off her shapely hips and runner's thighs.

"Now that's the one, ma. You'll crush the whole building if you rock that one," Marissa said. She was lying across a bed, surfing the internet on Pearl's laptop while Pearl tried on clothes.

Pearl gave the dress one last critical look then frowned. "Nah, I don't think it shows off enough boob." She cupped her breasts in her hands.

"Jesus, that's the third dress you've tried on since we been up here," Marissa said.

"That's why I bought five, to make sure I get it right," Pearl told her, unzipping the dress and wiggling out of it. She was a curvaceous girl, who had just over a handful of breasts, and shapely legs from years of running track in school.

"Girl, I would kill for that body. You can eat what you want and not gain a pound, but I gotta sweat for three days out of the week in the gym so I don't grow up to be my *abuelita*," Marissa joked.

"Good genes, baby." Pearl ran her hand over her flat stomach. "I wouldn't be too worried if I were you. I've seen Evelyn in a bathing suit and your mom has got a banging body!"

"That doesn't have anything to do with genes. That's all courtesy of Dr. Schwartz."

"Your mom had surgery? You lying!" Pearl couldn't believe it.

"Tits, tummy, and nose," Marissa rattled off.

"Wow, I'd have never known. Everything looks so natural."

"I should hope so. For what my mom has paid in plastic surgeries, I could've done two years in college."

"Well, it isn't like your dad doesn't have it to blow on her. As much money as he's made with my dad over the years, plus his regular job, I know y'all ain't hurting."

"No, we ain't hurting, but we ain't doing it like y'all . . . not at five percent," Marissa told her.

"Girl, what you talking about? I know Tito ain't in the life, but I know for a fact that him and my dad do a lot of legitimate business together. They're partners, right?"

At first Marissa thought she was joking, but the confused expression on Pearl's face said that she wasn't. "Mami, you can't possibly be that naive." She closed the laptop and sat up. "Pearl, have you never asked yourself how a man with dirty money can spend it in a legitimate establishment? It has to be cleaned first," she answered her own question.

"So you telling me Tito launders money for my dad?"

"Hell no! My dad ain't trying to fuck up an eight-figure annual salary and stock options over no bullshit. He's the go-between;

the guy who puts people like your father into a room with other people who know what to do with that kind of money."

"Wow, I'd have never thought Tito had that in him," Pearl said, trying to picture the man who had taken them camping in the summers moving in a room full of gangsters. It didn't fit.

"Exactly, and that's what makes him the perfect buffer. You mean to tell me you've been living in this house for eighteen years and you still don't know how shit works?" Marissa was curious.

"You know my dad keeps me out of his business."

"So does mine, but I'm too nosy not to know what's going on under my own roof," Marissa said.

Marissa had given Pearl some food for thought. She had known since she was a kid that her father didn't have a traditional job, and some of their gains were ill-gotten, but she had never cared to know anything beyond that. Pearl had always been raised to not ask questions, and until now it had been okay with her so long as she was provided for, but in light of the mounting tensions and whispers around her house lately, she began to wonder if maybe she should start paying more attention.

"So, any word from Ruby about tonight?" Marissa changed the subject, seeing that she had created an awkward moment with her revelation. "I spoke to her yesterday after school and she said she'll be here, but nothing after that. If you ask me I don't think she's going to make it. Her parents already had her on lockdown, and I hear that after they caught wind of what happened with me and Sheila they probably added extra security."

"Knowing them I wouldn't doubt it but don't be so quick to count Ruby out. My girl can get very resourceful when she needs to. We'll play it by ear."

"Well, whether she comes or not, it ain't gonna stop my fun. I plan on getting my swerve on!" Marissa declared.

"When do you not?" Pearl teased her. "I'm trying to do my thing too, but it's probably gonna be damn near impossible with my daddy and his friends there. I'll probably end up stuck with Knowledge or Power hovering over my shoulder all night."

"Speaking of Knowledge, what do you know about this chick he's supposed to be bringing tonight? From the way he moves in the streets, I always thought he was single."

"Me too. This is the first time I ever heard talk of him having a chick. I hope it ain't one of them hood-rat bitches from the neighborhood. You know I ain't trying to have no bum-ass bitches up in my shit," Pearl said.

"Knowledge don't strike me as the type to bring no ghetto ho around Big Stone. She's probably some fake bourgeois bitch who gonna be in there drinking wine with her pinkie out." Marissa faked the motion for emphasis.

"I don't care what kind of chick she is, so long as she stays in her lane and recognizes who the boss bitch is."

The ringing of the pink phone on Pearl's nightstand interrupted their conversation. She snatched the cordless from the base and looked at the caller ID. It was an unknown number. Still she sighed, as she knew who it was and what he was calling about.

Marissa read the distressed look on her face. *Who that?* she mouthed.

"You know who." Pearl rolled her eyes.

"Damn, that boy is determined." Marissa laughed.

"I ain't even picking up." Pearl moved to put the phone back on the base, but Marissa stopped her.

"Nah, I got it." Marissa snatched the phone from her before she could protest. "Stone residence," she answered.

"Ah . . . Pearl?" the voice stammered on the other end.

"No, this isn't Pearl. You wanna leave another message, or keep ringing my girl's phone on some loco shit?" she taunted him.

"Who is this? That crazy Spanish bitch Marissa? Stop playing with me and put Pearl on the phone!" he snapped.

"Bitch? Who you calling a bitch, wit' you ol' sprung ass? Pearl is busy and she's gonna be busy every time you call, so get yourself a clue and knock it the fuck off before you get fucked up!" Marissa shouted.

"Gimme." Pearl took the phone back from her. "Devonte, please stop calling me. I told you I ain't got shit to say to you."

"Pearl, I know I lost my temper the other night, but—"

"Lost your temper? More like lost your fucking mind. After that insane shit you pulled trying to snatch me off my block you're lucky I ain't got niggas at your crib right now, tossing your ass up. Boy, you got issues I ain't equipped to deal with. Do us both a favor and lose my number." She slammed the phone down. "This nigga is on my last nerves," she huffed.

"Why don't you just get your number changed?" Marissa asked.

"Because then I'd have to explain to my father why I want it changed," Pearl pointed out. "Why can't he just leave me alone?"

"The better question is, what were you doing behind closed doors that got him all out of his mind? My mother always told me good pussy is way more dangerous than a gun."

"Tell me about it." Pearl flopped on the bed next to Marissa.

"It's like ones you want to be rid of won't leave and the ones you want to keep won't stay. I attract all the wrong types of guys."

"The last one you met at the bar seemed cool. What was his name, Diamonds?" Marissa asked.

Pearl sucked her teeth. "Fuck that nigga."

"Wow, a few days ago he was all you could talk about. What brought on the sudden change?"

"He showed me who he really was." Pearl flipped open her phone and started scrolling through her call log.

CHAPTER ELEVEN

Diamonds sat cross-legged on the cot in his cell. His eyes were closed, and his breaths short and measured. He was trying to move as little as possible as to slow the poison working its way through his bloodstream. The fever had subsided a bit, but he could still feel the ache in his joints. Time was definitely not his friend in this situation.

Since he was a kid running barefoot through the swamps Diamonds had always been careful, thinking and rethinking every move before he made it. This is how he had been able to make it as far as he had. He was always one step ahead of his enemy, knowing what moves they would make before he did, but something had changed. He could think of a dozen people to point the finger at for his misfortune, but ultimately the blame was solely on him. He'd grown cocky and overconfident, buying into his own hype, and that's how a half-wit like Big Slim had been able to get the drop on him.

This raised another burning question in his head: How did Big Slim know where to find him after all this time? The obvious answer would've been Dip's snake ass. Dip was a former member of Diamonds' crew, who had stolen two kilos of heroin from them before they left New Orleans. Goldie had wanted to track him down and kill him for it, but Diamonds figured it wasn't worth the effort. They had more than enough dope to get them started and the two kilos hardly made a dent in their supply. He was sure Slim had tracked Dip down first, probably torturing him before ending his worthless life, but even so all Dip knew was that Diamonds and his crew were headed to Texas after leaving New Orleans. They had run through at least a half dozen cities before landing in New York and they never shared their real plans with any of the mercenaries they'd employed in those cities. The only people who knew their final destination were those in their immediate circle, so that meant somebody was playing both sides.

Footfalls in the hall outside his cell pulled Diamonds from his thoughts. He quickly slipped back under the tattered blanket and pretended to be asleep. The door opened and Diamonds made out the silhouette of a man too big to be Brother Minister, but not big enough to be Big Slim. The man paused in the doorway and spoke to someone Diamonds couldn't see. There were only two of them as near as he could tell. Not the best odds, but not the worse either.

"Rise and shine, sleeping beauty." The man flicked on the overhead light.

Diamonds squinted, trying to clear his vision. The man standing over him was one of his captors, the one he had come to know as Blue. Diamonds had been hoping it was the other one, Tariq. Tariq had been especially cruel in his treatment of Diamonds and he was hoping to repay the favor sooner than later. Diamonds sat up slowly, as if he were just coming out of a deep slumber. "Top of the morning, boys . . . or is it afternoon? Maybe evening? When you been in the dark for a time, one feels the same as the other," he said with a scratchy throat.

"Somebody wants to see you," Blue told him. "Now I'm gonna cut you loose and you're gonna play nice. If you don't, I'm gonna put you in a world of hurt." He inched toward Diamonds with the key to his shackle.

"Your rules, I'm just playing the game." Diamonds flashed him a weak smile.

"Quit being scared. That boy is in such bad shape I doubt he could wipe his own ass let alone hurt you," someone called from the doorway. Diamonds recognized the voice as Tariq's.

"Shut up, and just make sure you cover me," Blue said over his shoulder. Keeping his eyes on Diamonds, he knelt down and removed the shackle. "Now get up," he ordered.

Diamonds pushed off the bed and stood. He rocked once before crashing to the floor as if his legs couldn't support him. "Apologies, I must've left my dancing shoes in my other luggage."

Blue looked down at Diamonds in disgust. "This nigga is in worse shape than I thought. What the fuck did y'all do to him?" he asked Tariq.

"That wasn't on me. I knocked him around a little bit, but it was Big Slim who took it to him with that funny-looking knife. Maybe he'll bleed out and we can be done with his ass," Tariq said.

"Get you country ass up." Blue snatched Diamonds to his feet. He threatened to fall again, but Blue was able to steady him by draping his arm around his neck.

"I don't think I like you much. Brother Minister is a heap more polite than you two," Diamonds said, swaying against Blue like he was drunk.

"Well, your new bridge partner is out handling something for Big Slim, so you're stuck with us," Blue told him as began half dragging Diamonds toward the door.

"Jesus, I can smell him from over here." Tariq fanned the stench coming from Diamonds' soiled body.

"Why don't you help me carry him instead of complaining?"

"Slim ain't paying me enough to touch that rank muthafucka," Tariq said.

Diamonds listened to the men argue back and forth while waiting for his window of opportunity. He was tempted to make his move early, but had to wait for just the right time or it would be for nothing. When Blue dropped his guard to adjust Diamonds' weight, he knew it was time.

Blue was caught totally by surprise when Diamonds grabbed him in a headlock and yanked his head back. From his waistband Diamonds drew the bedspring he had worked loose while he and Brother Minister had been talking and hooked the sharp edge into the soft flesh of Blue's throat.

"Shoot this nigga!" Blue shouted at Tariq.

The stunned Tariq drew his gun, but couldn't get a clear shot.

"Try it if you got a mind to, but I doubt that you're that good of a shot. Even on the slim chance that you are, I'll rip this nigga open before you take me down," Diamonds hissed. Tariq lowered his gun. "That's more like it. Now the first thing you gonna do is kick that gun down the hall where it can't do no harm and then you're gonna tuck yourself in that cell." He would've rather had the gun, but there was no way he could get to it without releasing his grip on Blue.

Reluctantly, Tariq did as he was told and kicked the gun away. Keeping his eyes on Diamonds he stepped into the cell. "Big Slim is gonna kill you for this."

"If he was smart he'd have done that the moment he snatched me," Diamonds taunted him before kicking the door closed behind him. "How we get outta here?" he asked Blue.

"I ain't telling you shit!" Blue spat.

"Is that right?" Diamonds pulled the bedspring, widening the tear in Blue's throat.

"A'ight, a'ight!" Blue yelled. "Down the hall and to the right."

"Let's go." Diamonds started pulling him down the hallway. They had made it halfway to the door Blue had directed him to when it opened and a man stepped through it. For a half second Diamonds took his eyes off Blue, but it was all the time needed to dash his plan to hell. Pain shot through his entire midsection as Blue's elbow shot into it, opening up his stitches and causing him to lose his grip on the bedspring. Blue followed with an elbow to his jaw that would've put him on his back had it not been for the wall holding him up. Things were going south very quickly.

The man who had distracted him now entered the fray and grabbed Diamonds from behind in a reverse bear hug. He struggled, but between his injuries and the poison didn't have the strength to break the hold. Diamonds watched as Blue stalked toward him with murder in his eyes.

"I'll bet you thought that shit was cute, huh?" Blue sneered. He reached up and yanked the bedspring from his neck, dripping blood down his shirt. He took a few seconds to examine the weapon. "Nice little shank you made here," he said before slashing Diamonds across the face with it. "Pretty sharp too. Hold that nigga up."

While the minion held Diamonds, Blue started waling on him, paying special attention to his injured stomach. Diamonds coughed blood onto Blue's shoes, which only seemed to make him angrier. He slugged Diamonds over and over, while the minion holding him cheered Blue on. Diamonds was in so much pain that he wanted to lay down and die, but he knew death was a mercy Slim wouldn't allow him until he was finished with his little game.

"Please . . . no more," Diamonds begged.

"Don't quit on me now, tough guy." Blue tilted his head up so he could get a clean shot at Diamonds' chin. When he fired the blow, Diamonds moved his head to one side and Blue ended up slugging the minion instead, causing him to lose his grip on Diamonds.

Diamonds fired his head backward, knocking out two of the minion's teeth and freeing himself. Without missing a beat, he kicked Blue square in the nuts and put him down. Summoning what strength he had left Diamonds bolted.

The minion drew his gun and prepared to fire, but Blue stopped him. "Don't waste the bullet. He ain't going nowhere."

Diamonds half ran, half staggered down the hallway toward the door. He was bleeding out, winded, and in terrible pain but had to keep going. He pushed through the door, which let him out into another hallway. He pressed his back against the door, looking around frantically trying to get his bearings. To his left there was a stairwell leading up to another door. Through the small window in it he could see the sun shining. *Freedom!* the word exploded in his head. He listened for a moment, expecting to hear Blue and the minion on his heels, but there was nothing. *Why weren't they chasing him?* Pushing the question from his head, Diamonds lurched forward and hit the stairs.

When he reached the door at the top, he tried the handle and prayed that it wasn't locked. For once, God listened to him. When Diamonds stumbled out into the afternoon sun and took stock of his surroundings, the sliver of hope he'd been holding on to drained away. He now understood why Blue and the minion hadn't bothered to chase him. The whole time he'd assumed that Big Slim was holding him in a basement or warehouse, but he had been wrong. The only way Diamonds would be escaping this prison was on a boat.

"You shouldn't have done that," Diamonds heard someone behind him say before something heavy slammed into his head and everything went black.

CHAPTER TWELVE

After dropping Domo off at the train station, Buda and the rest of his gang rolled back to the stash house, which was a one-story house located in the Bronx. The owner of the house was a drug addict who would let them have the run of the place so long as they kept her high. After all that had gone on, Buda didn't think it wise that they continue to use the old one in Harlem because of all the heat they had been drawing lately. It was the only thing they seemed to unanimously agree on lately.

"Dump this ride and then meet us back here when you're done," Buda told Lucky as he gathered up their spoils and the pillowcase of guns.

"Man, why do I always have to do the grunt work?" Lucky complained. Ever since he had arrived in New York he'd either been the designated driver or errand boy and he was getting a little tired of it.

"Because I say so," Buda replied. "If you got a problem with your position in this crew, I'm more than willing to give you a pistol and let you get dirty with the rest of us."

"A'ight, man," Lucky relented. He didn't like the idea of letting the money out of his sight before he got his cut, but he liked the idea of arguing with Buda even less.

"Just as I thought. Don't fret over it, homie. Your cut will be here waiting for you when you get back," Buda said as if he could read Lucky's mind.

Buda used they key he had been given and let himself into the house. The first thing he noticed was the unmistakable chemical smell of crack smoke hanging in the air. That meant the lady of the house, Mousey, was home. When he rounded the corner in the living room they found it a mess as usual. The carpet looked like it hadn't been vacuumed in weeks, and beer bottles lined the coffee table. On the couch were Mousey and her on-again-off-again boyfriend Tick. He was fast sleep with his head lolled back, while Mousey had her face buried in his lap with his dick hanging halfway out of her mouth. Apparently, she had passed out in the middle of giving him a blow job. It was the most comical thing Buda had ever seen, so he decided to have some fun with them.

"Hold this." Buda handed the bag to Willie while he crept up on the sleeping crack fiends. He raised his massive hands and clapped them thunderously over their heads.

The sound scared Mousey awake and she reflexively clamped her teeth together over Tick's flaccid penis. Pain shot through his member, causing him to leap to his feet, knocking her onto the coffee table and spilling what was left in the beer bottles onto the floor. Abandoning Mousey, Tick ran for the window thinking the spot was being raided when he spotted Buda doubled over laughing.

"That shit wasn't funny, man," Tick said, checking his dick to make sure it was still attached.

"Shit, it gave me a good laugh," Buda said. "What the fuck I tell y'all about getting high up here in the living room making the spot hot? You wanna blast off, take that shit in the basement."

"Last time I checked, this was my house." Mousey was finally pulling herself up off the floor.

"A house that they were about to foreclose on until I stepped into the picture," Buda reminded her. "Now stop mouthing off and get your ass in the basement like a good little dog, so me and my people can talk business."

Mousey and Tick gathered their things so they could move their party to the basement. As they were passing, Buda heard Mousey mumble, "Asshole," under her breath.

"Fuck did you just say?" Buda asked, the amused grin suddenly gone from his face.

"She didn't say nothing, man," Tick lied.

"Was I talking to you, nigga?" Buda snapped. He moved in on Mousey. "I asked you to repeat yourself."

"C'mon, Buda. I was just joking. You know how we do." Mousey tried to laugh it off.

"No doubt, baby. We all good." Buda flashed his crocodile grin. Just when everyone thought the moment would pass, Buda slapped Mousey across the face. The blow landed with so much force that she bounced off the wall before hitting the floor. "Junkie whore, don't you ever in your life disrespect me in front of my people." He kicked her in the ribs viciously.

"What the fuck is going on out here?" Hank came out of the kitchen, gun drawn.

"Nothing, man. Just cracking some jokes, and a few ribs." Buda laughed.

"Must you be an asshole all your life?" Hank shoved him away from Mousey, then knelt to check on her. "You okay?"

"Yeah, I'm straight," Mousey lied. She wasn't sure what hurt worse, the slap or the kick, but she was in a world of pain.

Hank helped Mousey to her feet and pressed a small package of drugs into her palm. "I'll hook you up with a little something heavier later on, okay?" Mousey just nodded. Hank then turned to Tick, who was just standing there, scared shitless. "Make yourself useful and take her downstairs, you piece of shit. What kinda nigga won't lift a finger to protect his woman?"

Tick lowered his head in shame. He wanted to help her, he truly did, but wanted no part of Buda's wrath. He reached for Mousey, but she pulled away and descended the basement stairs. Tick gave Hank one last shameful look before following her.

"Hank, why the fuck you always sticking up for that junkie bitch?" Buda asked.

"Just because she strung out don't give you no right to treat her like a dog!" Hank snapped. "Besides, with all the dirt we do up in this house the last thing we need is her mad enough to call the police on us. We'll all be fucked then."

"That bitch knows if she even think about calling the cops I'll kill her and everybody she loves," Buda promised.

All Hank could do was shake his head because he knew Buda was a man who was beyond reasoning with. The threat of Mousey calling the police wasn't likely, but Hank would never reveal his real motive for always looking out for the junkie. Hank had a soft spot for Mousey because he used to be her. Few other than Diamonds knew about Hank's battle with addiction. There was a dark period in his life when he had done some things he wasn't proud of in order to get his fix.

"Y'all snag that bag?" Buda asked.

"Yeah, I was in the kitchen repacking all the shit before you started your Ike Turner shit," Hank told him.

"Good man. Where Goldie and Snake?" Buda asked.

"Goldie had something to take care of and Snake caught it in the battle. Dude we moved on got the drop on him," Hank lied. He didn't tell Buda what really happened because the last thing they needed was to create more tension among the group.

Buda shrugged. "What's a war without its casualties? Let's go finish bagging this shit up."

Vita sat perched on the washing machine near the kitchen window lost in her own thoughts, while the men helped Hank repackage the drugs they had stolen from Big Stone's runner. Lucky had returned from dumping the car and was leaning against the stove, rolling up a blunt. Every so often he would cast a distrustful look at Buda, who was laughing and popping shit like he didn't have a care in the world. Vita had seen that look before, and she had a good idea what was going through his mind. He would bear some watching.

In truth, she didn't particularly care for any of the new faces who had joined their crew. Even when they were still pulling capers in New Orleans none of them, with the exception of One-eye Willie, had ever really been a part of what they had going on. To Vita the men were just little more than muscle, loyal to whoever was paying them at the time, and if Buda wasn't careful the same snakes he had brought into their home would end up biting him, which might not be such a bad thing.

Buda had never been the easiest man to get along with, but he had gotten far worse when he became the leader. Under Diamonds their moves had been calculated and quiet, but Buda lacked that same tact and patience. It the week since Diamonds had gone missing, Buda had caused a shit storm in the street. Instead of taking his time eating the meal Diamonds had laid on the table for them, as had been the plan, Buda had been killing and taking more out of greed than necessity, trying to gobble it all down at once. He was a mindless brute who had inherited more power than he was capable of handling, and Vita had a bad feeling that it would only be a matter of time before his bullshit got them all either killed or thrown in prison for the rest of their lives.

What bothered Vita more than Buda risking their lives unnecessarily was how he had taken Diamonds' disappearance. On the surface, he appeared to be just as broken up over it as the rest of them, but it didn't feel right. His grief seemed rehearsed, less than genuine, and that struck her as odd, knowing how close they had been. It was possible that Vita had been reading too much into it, but her gut said she was on to something. Either way, she would be watching him like a hawk until she got to the bottom of it.

Roughly two hours had passed and there was still no sign of Domo, and she didn't know if she was more irritated or worried. She hadn't missed Buda's insinuation that Domo was going to see another chick, which shouldn't have been her concern, but it bothered her. The more time she spent around the youngster, the more he was beginning to grow on her, which is why she had started to push him away.

Vita had never been a woman big on attachments of any kind. As a child she and her family never lived anywhere for more than a few months to a year before getting evicted or having to relocate due to something one of her junkie parents did. It was always a new neighborhood, new school, and new friends, and this taught her not to hold on to anything too tight because it wouldn't last. This was especially true when it came to relationships. Diamonds had been the closest thing to a boyfriend she ever had and even with him the lows outweighed the highs. He treated her like little more than a toy to be taken in or out of the box whenever he felt like playing with it. Still, she loved him as she had no other in her life . . . and then Domo came into the picture.

The hooligan from Newark was a conundrum that she hadn't quite figured out yet. He was young, broke, and almost comically inexperienced when it came to lovemaking, but he was genuine, which was something Vita wasn't used to. For all his flaws he seemed to genuinely care for her and it scared Vita shitless. After what she had been through with Diamonds over the years Vita was emotionally damaged and no longer trusted her heart to be able to lead her in the right direction. What if she let her guard down and gave herself to Domo, only for him to toy with her as Diamonds had? Then again, what if she pushed him away, only later to find she had robbed herself of a blessing? There were so many unanswered questions in her head that it made her dizzy.

"Man, I gotta admit that I was a little skeptical when you hit me about coming to New York, but after what I've seen so far I should've got out of dodge with you niggas years ago," One-eye Willie said, looking at all the drugs on the table.

"This is only the start, my man. We're about to own this city!" Buda boasted.

"Yeah, this is a pretty sweet situation Diamonds set up. Too bad he ain't hear to reap the benefits of his groundwork," Lucky said offhandedly. The room suddenly got quiet, as he had hit a sore spot. "I'm sorry. I didn't mean to—"

"It's all good, Lucky. The wound is still pretty fresh, but time and cash heals all." Buda slipped a rubber band around a stack of money and tossed it on the table.

"So, y'all plan a home-going yet?" Willie asked.

"Home-going for the dead. We ain't got no proof Diamonds passed on yet, and until we do I'd appreciate it if you boys wouldn't be so quick to put him in the ground!" Vita said angrily.

"Vita, you still on that?" Buda looked at her. "The writing is on the wall, baby girl. I don't wanna believe it either, but it's been over a week and no sign of him."

"I tend to agree with Vita," Hank added. "Even if it went as Buda suggests, and fools did manage to catch him slipping, ain't no way he would've gone quietly and for damn sure not alone. I spoke to our guy on the inside and ain't been no new casualties reported besides the few bodies we laid down."

"You tip him off to the fact that Diamonds gone missing?" Buda asked suspiciously. He already knew the answer, but wanted to see how Hank would play it.

"Nah, I ain't no fool. I just made some inquiries about the state of their crew. Played it off like I was doing recon for the big move," Hank told him.

"Smart man. We still don't know how far we can trust these New York niggas, and I don't want them knowing more about what we got going on than they need to." Buda had learned a long time ago not to let his left hand know what his right was doing, and both of his had been quite busy lately.

"Maybe somebody snatched him and he's being held somewhere," Vita suggested.

"Then where's the ransom note?" Buda asked. "Listen, do y'all think I haven't been up day and night looking at this from all possible angles? Don't nobody wanna be wrong about this more than I do, but all we got is what's in front of us. Regardless of what your inside man is telling you, it don't change the fact that someone has done us a great injustice. Maybe it was Big Stone, and maybe it was somebody else. I say we make 'em all bleed to be sure our brother's passing is felt!"

"Now that's some shit I can get with!" Willie said excitedly. "We been knocking soldiers out since we arrived in New York. When do we get to hunt the big game?"

"Sooner than you think, my friend." Buda said with a sly grin. "Now if we're all done here, I gotta head back to Manhattan. I got a date with a bitch who's just dying for me to stick this cock to her."

"I'll ride with you," Vita said, much to Buda's surprise.

"I never figured you down for a three-way, but if you're game so am I," Buda told her suggestively. He was hoping to scare her off so she'd change her mind about tagging along.

"Don't flatter yourself, fat boy. I left my ride downtown, remember?"

"Right." Buda chuckled. "For a minute, I thought you'd finally opened your mind up to a Buda sandwich."

"Not on my worse day. I'll wait for you outside. There's too much testosterone in here for my taste." Vita walked out of the kitchen.

"I swear, that girl is even more sour than I remember," Willie said once she had gone.

"Probably since she ain't had a good dicking since Diamonds," Hank joked.

"So you say. Ain't nobody but me been peeping how close she playing that young boy?" Willie asked.

"Who, Domo? Nah, man. They been flirting a bit, but I doubt it go further than that. His flesh probably way too tender for her fangs," Hank pointed out.

"You say that because you don't see what I see. When y'all gonna stop doubting my vision?" Willie pointed to his glass eye.

"Well, ask that marble rolling around in your head when you're finally gonna get laid. I think you're the only one who ain't had no pussy since we been in New York," Lucky teased him.

"I'm gonna leave all you dry-dick niggas to it." Buda got up from the table. "Hank, walk me out."

"What's on your head?" Hank asked once they were out of earshot of the others.

"How much you trust our guy on the inside?"

Hank shrugged. "About as much as I can trust any muthafucka who'll double-cross his own. I thought it stank to high shit from the moment Diamonds brought that janky nigga Born to the table. I trust his partner Rolling even less. Any man his age who dresses like he stepped out of a nineties rap video gotta have some funny shit with him."

"You having second thoughts about the deal?" Buda asked.

"Second and third," Hank admitted. "I'm thinking we should put this deal on hold until we can figure out exactly where everyone stands."

"Normally I'd agree but the ball is already in play. Doodles and his people are supposed to be hitting us with the first official shipment tomorrow night," Buda informed him.

This surprised Hank because he wasn't aware they'd locked in a delivery date yet. "Well, when were you planning on telling us about it?"

"I just found out this morning," Buda lied. "Can't blame them for being anxious. The lane is wide open right now with Pana out of the way, so I figure this is as good a time as any to lay to all the territory we spilled all that blood to clean out."

"Buda, don't you think you're moving a little fast?"

"No faster than Diamonds. Hell, look at how quick we swept through Miami. Diamonds took that bitch in half the time it's taking us to move on New York."

"Diamonds also had a plan in place before we did anything. You're just reacting to what's being thrown out there," Hank pointed out.

"What more planning do we need than to take all this shit and lay out whoever touched our brother in the process? You starting to sound like an old wet nurse, Hank. Maybe it's time for you to step back and let the fresh blood handle the dirty work."

"Or maybe it's time for you to think about what's good for this crew, instead of just what's good for Buda," Hank shot back. "Look here, boss; I know you the chief of the shit now. It's your right by chain of command, and I might not like it but I respect it. But you know this ain't how we move. One mind," Hank tapped his forehead with his index finger, "one heart," he tapped Buda's chest with the same finger. "That's how Diamonds set this thing up to work."

"And look where it got him," Buda replied. "Hank, you a wise old bird and the best adviser a man can ask for in matters of money, but we at war. This is my area of expertise, so let me do what I do. Now if you don't like the way I'm running this thing, you more than welcome to bring your complaints to the big table and challenge me for leadership. Just know that nothing short of death is gonna take me from this position now that I finally have it. You feel me?"

"Nah, I don't feel you, but it is what it is. You the chief now, right?" Hank's voice was laced with sarcasm. "If there's nothing else, I best get these drugs to the stash houses."

"Actually, nah. That coke ain't going to our spots uptown. It's going to Newark. I promised it to Domo and his people," Buda informed him.

"Another executive decision, huh?" Hank asked sarcastically. "Since when you start trying to look out for Domo? You know you can't stand him."

"I ain't gotta like him for him to be useful. Right now them young dudes is hungry, so why not set 'em to work? It ain't gonna do nothing but make the team richer."

"Right, Buda the team player," Hank said dryly. Buda was heaping the bullshit on so thick that the stench threatened to choke him.

"Have Lucky or Willie drop it off to them whenever they get a chance."

"Whatever you say, boss. Since I'm off the clock, I'm gonna

go check my bitch and get something to eat. That is, if it's okay with you, chief?"

"Hank, get the fuck outta here before you make me do something stupid," Buda grunted. It seemed that Hank was challenging his authority more and more lately, and Buda didn't like it. Hank was an elder statesman in their crew and his word carried a lot of weight. If he started putting ideas in the heads of the others it could complicate the plan Buda had so carefully laid out. Buda couldn't have that. Hank had always been a good friend to Buda and Diamonds, but in the new order of things a man like him was too dangerous to run around unchecked. Since Hank couldn't seem to fall in line, maybe it was time for him to simply fall.

CHAPTER THIRTEEN

Vita sat outside on the hood of Buda's car, watching the exchange between him and Hank through the side window of the house. She couldn't hear what they were saying, but from Hank's body language she didn't feel like it was a friendly conversation.

When Buda came out of the house his mood seemed darker, if that was even possible for someone who always seemed to be angry. "Everything okay with you?"

"Right as rain, baby girl." Buda snickered, as if he had made a joke to which only he knew the punchline. "Let's make a move." He jumped behind the wheel.

"So, that looked to be a pretty big score Goldie and them took off," Vita said once they were in traffic.

"Big enough. Most of it I'm sending to Newark for Domo and L.A. to move, but even off what we keep it'll be at least a few days before we need to see Eddie again," Buda told her.

"Speaking of him, anybody seen him? I noticed he's been MIA since Diamonds disappeared," Vita pointed out.

"Knowing him, he probably thinks we're looking at him over what happened to Diamonds," Buda said.

"Why aren't we?" Vita asked. "He was hotter than fish grease that Diamonds cut him out of that heroin deal. I wouldn't put it past him to try and pull a ho move."

"It's possible, but I doubt it. We're putting money in his pocket off this coke shit so it wouldn't really make sense for him to slit his own throat," Buda said. In truth the thought had crossed his mind, but he didn't want Vita to know it. Eddie had cut off all contact with Buda, dealing with him only through middle men whenever the crew needed to re-up. If he shared this with Vita or the any of the others they'd likely want to go at him with guns blazing, but Buda still needed Eddie.

"I'd be willing to bet my left tit that Eddie knows something about all this shit. I think I'm gonna take a few of the boys and pay him a little visit."

"Best let sleeping dogs lie, at least for right now, V."

"Buda, you know don't nothing move in this city that he don't know about. I ain't saying we gotta press him, but at the very least it's a conversation that needs to be had."

"You right, and I'm two steps ahead of you on it. Just trust in your boy that I got this under control," Buda assured her. "I need to have a chat with him before this dope comes in anyway, so I can make sure there ain't gonna be no misunderstanding when we open up shop."

"Misunderstanding?" Vita gave him a look. "If I recall correctly, Diamonds already set him straight. We was welcome to them blocks we killed Pana for, so long as we bought cocaine from

Eddie's people. That dope plug Diamonds came up on is a separate issue, and Eddie got no claim or say on it."

"Still, best play nice until we figure out where everyone stands," Buda told her. Little did she know Buda was planning on baking a cake for Eddie's arrogant ass too. Buda hated Eddie, because he failed to show Eddie the same respect as he had Diamonds. He treated Buda like a worker, and it irritated him. He'd thought about just out-right killing him, but that would still leave his uncle Michael to deal with, and Buda's wasn't quite ready to handle a fish that big . . . at least not yet.

"Seems like that's all we been doing lately, playing," Vita said with an attitude.

"Come on, V. Don't you go getting all sour on me now too. I'm having a hard enough time adjusting to this new position, and it don't make it no easier when it feel like everybody bucking against me."

Vita spared him a glance, but her face hadn't softened.

"Baby girl, I don't wanna be big chief no more than any of you want me running things, but it don't change what is. Why do you think Diamonds made me his second instead of Hank, or even Goldie? Because he knew when the time came I'd be the one who was able to tuck his feelings and do what was best for this crew. Diamonds was a damn fine leader, and there ain't no way I'll ever be able to bring the things to the table that he did, which is why I gotta run this thing as I see fit. But at the end of the day we still a team; one mind and one heart," he repeated Hank's words. "Trust me, it's all gonna work out."

The two rode in silence for the next few miles. If Buda's speech had gotten through to Vita, she showed no signs of it. He had known from the beginning that next to Goldie, she would be the hardest of the crew to sway to his side. She'd had her head shoved up Diamonds' ass for so long that she could probably still smell his shit. He could sponsor her on a one-way trip to join her former lover, but he still needed Vita.

"Do you believe it?" Vita finally broke her silence.

"Believe what?"

"That stuff you were saying about Diamonds being dead?"

Buda thought on the question. "I don't want to, but ain't no other explanation. Our boy is dead and gone, and I'm willing to bet if we dig deep enough we'll find that blood on the hands of none other than Big Stone," he said venomously.

"Why are you so sure that Big Stone was behind it? You got an all-seeing eye like Willie now?" Vita asked suspiciously. She hadn't missed the fact that Buda had been not so subtly pushing them in that direction.

"Look at the chain of events. We start pushing fools out the game, then Diamonds starts catting around with the daughter of the potential opposition right before he goes missing." Buda shook his head. "Ain't all that much coincidence in the world."

"I knew that prissy bitch was gonna be trouble!" Vita spat, thinking back to the first night she had seen Pearl at Pops's bar. She knew she hated her from the moment she laid eyes on her. Not because Diamonds was sniffing around her, he chased pussy all the time. But it was the first time since Vita had known him that she had seen Diamonds look at a woman the way she always wished he'd looked at her.

"You and me both," Buda agreed. "I tried to tell him—hell, we all tried to tell him—but you know how Diamonds is when he gets his sights set on something. I ain't seen him that bent out of shape since Bleu."

Vita snorted at the mention of Diamonds' first, and some said only, true love. "That evil bitch worked a spell, so I can understand why he was so crazy over her. What Pearl got that's so special besides a young, tight pussy?"

"Sometimes that's all it takes," Buda said honestly.

"Well, if her fuck-ass daddy did have something to do with it I'm gonna cut his head off personally, and then I'm gonna carve that fast-ass baby girl of his up real nice," Vita promised.

"That's the Vita I know," Buda placed his hand on her thigh. "Say, I know losing Diamonds hit you harder than anyone else. If you ever need a ear to bend, or maybe something more, I'm here for you." He began sliding his hand farther up her thigh.

"Buda, you must of fell and bumped your damn skull." Vita slapped his hand away. "I'm broken up, not desperate."

"Damn, you act like I'm an ugly nigga or something," Buda said, clearly offended by her rejection.

"Physical appearance ain't got shit to do with it. It's what's lurking in that black heart of yours that's gonna always keep you at a distance. Besides, all you trying to do is fuck. I seen how you move with them other gals."

"That's because they ain't you," Buda said honestly. "Girl, you know I been crushing on you since the first day we met. Remember that?"

Vita laughed. "How could I? Especially when y'all came with plans on killing me."

It seemed like ages since Vita had first become a part of their band of misfits. Back then Diamonds and the others were just starting to get their weight up, but were starting to become quite notorious around the city. They had a young boy who they had moving dime bags for them down near Bourbon Street. It was slow money, but during Mardi Gras they made a nice piece of change off the tourists. On the final night of the parade, which was their most lucrative, the young boy came back to the spot beat all to hell with a story about having been robbed by someone called V.

Diamonds didn't think twice before arming up and rolling to where the young boy told him V was known to hang out. Buda and John-Boy were with him. When they got to the block there was a cluster of guys posted up shooting dice along with a young girl. By then Diamonds was making a reputation for himself as a killer, so the boys knew they were in trouble when they saw him walk up. They all appeared scared shitless, except the girl.

"You little grasshoppers know who I be?" Diamonds asked the young boys. They all nodded nervously. "Then you should know what happens to those foolish enough to steal from me, *yeah*? Because I'm still in a good mood from the day's activities, I'm gonna give you a break and not punish all you lil niggas." The boys breathed a collective sigh of relief. "Just tell me which one of you niggas is V, and I'll take my business up with him."

The boys all looked back and forth between each other as if they were trying to figure out who among them would wear the blame.

"Well, since y'all seem to have a problem remembering your names," Diamonds pulled out the biggest gun they had ever seen, "everybody gets the business."

"I'm, V." The girl stepped forward. She was scared, but trying her best to hide it.

Diamonds studied her. "Girl, you got a big heart, I'll give you that. But why you trying to protect a boyfriend who won't stand up for himself? And what kinda nigga let's his lady volunteer to take his bullet?" He looked over the boys.

"No, I really am V," the girl insisted. "It's short for Vita."

Diamonds cast a disappointed glance at his worker. When he had recounted the story of the robbery he had omitted the part about it being a girl who had jacked him. "Girl, you can't be no more than one hundred pounds on your best day. You expect me to believe you done this deed all by your lonesome?" he still wasn't quite convinced.

"I don't care what you believe, I'm telling you what happened," she said defiantly, trying to find her courage.

"She's a real spitfire," Buda chimed in.

"Indeed she is," Diamonds agreed. He paused for a few ticks as if he were weighing what to do next. Vita was dusty and a little rough around the edges, but beneath it she had a beauty about her that stirred something in Diamonds. "Tell me something, Ms. Vita, do you know what pirates did to people in the old days who stole from them?"

Vita shrugged. "I don't know."

"Well, I'll tell you. They either made them walk the plank," Diamonds brandished his gun, "or shanghaied them into their pirate crew. Which one will it be for you, Ms. Vita?"

"I ain't never been so scared in my life," Vita recalled.

"But you stood tall. I know then that you was gonna grow up to be a special lady. Only reason I didn't push up on you then was because Diamonds ol' thirsty ass got to you first."

"And so you figure now that Diamonds is gone it's your turn at the plate?" Vita saw where the conversation was going.

"Damn, baby, you know I ain't mean it like that. V, you been the queen of this crew since the beginning. You strong, and you crazy as hell, which are the two things I love most about you. You stood by Diamonds when he was chief, and now I'm hoping you stand by me."

Vita had to take a minute to see if Buda was joking, but from the look on his face he wasn't. This was the first time since his little brother was killed that she had ever seen him show anything close to human emotion. "Buda, I'm sorry but this can never be."

Hurt flashed in Buda's eyes. "Why, because I ain't Diamonds?"

"No, but that's part of it," Vita admitted. "I done been through enough with men in my short life to know that from here on I gotta make wiser choices with my heart."

"That the same thing you told Domo? You ain't even let Diamonds get cold in the grave before you let him have a taste." Buda hadn't meant to say it, but she'd hurt him and he wanted to hurt her back.

Vita's sour expression returned. "Beneath those pretty words lies the same old Buda. Man, you can let me out on the corner. I'll take a taxi the rest of the way."

"Vita, I'm sorry. I didn't—"

"I said let me the fuck out!"

"All right, keep your damn shirt on." Buda waited for a break in traffic and pulled over at the curb. Vita reached for the door, but he hit the locks. "Look, girl, I hope you ain't taking this too personal. We still got money to get and I'd hate for some misplaced words to make things bad between us."

"Buda, shit already bad between us. Personally, I ain't got no script for you. But as far as that paper goes, I'll be wherever I need to be whenever I need to be there, as always." Vita unlocked the door and got out, slamming it behind her.

That went far worse than Buda had expected. He had been scheming on running up on Vita for years, but that cock-blocking ass Diamonds had always been in the way. Secretly, he had always been jealous of Diamonds and Vita's relationship. Diamonds was a piece of shit who stuck his dick into whomever he pleased whenever he pleased, while Vita turned a blind eye to it. Her weakness for Diamonds made him sick, and he tried to punch holes in things between them whenever he could, yet Vita remained loyal to him, even in death.

Fuck it and fuck her, Buda thought to himself. Once Buda's hold was absolute, she would have no choice but to see that he was the better man. If she didn't, she would find herself expendable, as would anyone who represented a threat to his master plan. It was time to start cleaning house. With this in mind, he set out to meet with his new business partners.

CHAPTER FOURTEEN

The meeting was scheduled to go down in Brooklyn, at a Cuban restaurant off Washington Street. He'd told Doodles that he selected the spot because it was their turf, but of course that was a lie. Buda had chosen the restaurant because it was public and the police patrolled the area heavily. That would keep everyone honest.

When he arrived, he noticed T.J. was already there. He was pacing back and forth, pulling on a cigarette nervously. He was probably scared to death. T.J. was Diamonds' cousin and had been the crew's liaison in New York City. He had been the one who brokered the deal between the crew and Eddie, and had been fielding the situation with Doodles and his crew in Diamonds' absence. Buda had never liked T.J. because he felt the boy was all mouth and no action. He was soft, and Buda didn't like weak people. The only reason he hadn't killed him yet was because T.J. was still of value to his cause. The moment he closed the deal with Doodles, T.J. was going for a dirt nap.

"Sup, lil nigga?" Buda greeted T.J. when he stepped onto the curb. T.J. was nearly a foot taller than Buda so he had to look up when he spoke to him.

"Chilling." T.J. ignored the insult. "Everybody is inside already."

Buda looked at his watch. "Am I late?"

"No, they showed up early. I don't know, Buda. I'm getting a funny vibe about all this."

"Nigga, stop being so fucking scared. Everything is going to be fine." Buda slapped him on the back harder than he needed to and proceeded inside the restaurant.

"So, any word on my cousin yet?" T.J. fell in step behind Buda.

"Nah, man. Still quiet. My money is still on Big Stone finding out he was fucking his daughter and having him clipped," Buda told him.

"Yeah, about that . . . before you got here I was talking to Born. He says he hasn't heard anything, but for some reason I don't believe him," T.J. said.

"And why would he tell you even if he did? The man has already proven he's a snake by agreeing to double-cross his boss. Don't worry, T.J., once we knock the big man off, everybody else is going to get what they got coming shortly after. You got my word on that," Buda said seriously.

It wasn't hard to spot their party. Rolling stuck out like a sore thumb, wearing an oversize green and yellow baseball jersey and matching hat. Several cheap-looking gold chains dangled from his neck. The man had to be at least fifty-something years old, but still dressed like a teenager. He looked like a damn fool, but Buda had learned firsthand that looks could be deceiving when it came to Rolling Stone. He was the brother of Big Stone, and the man who probably hated him most of all for reasons only known to him. Next to him was Doodles, a tall Jamaican cat. With his matted dreadlocks and a shaggy beard that covered almost his entire face, he looked like a mountaineer. He was a known killer throughout the streets of Brooklyn and the man who would allegedly be fronting the heroin Buda and his crew would distribute. Last was Born, the turncoat, and an old-school cat who hustled drugs out of Queens. Until recently he had been one of Big Stone's street bosses, then he got tired of eating the crumbs off the big man's plate and decided he was entitled to a plate of his own. He was now one of the three-headed monsters who would help Buda knock the old-timer out of the box once and for all. There was another man with them, one Buda didn't recognize. He was a young, dark-skinned dude who was dressed in a black suit and white shirt. He reminded Buda of one of the Muslims he always saw peddling papers on 125th Street. His presence was a surprise and Buda didn't like surprises.

"Who's your friend?" Buda asked Born.

"This is Minister, an associate of ours. He's up from Florida to help us move things along," Born told him.

"Florida, huh?" Buda eyed him suspiciously. "I spent a bit of time down there. Maybe our paths have crossed?"

"I doubt it," Minister said, sipping his water.

"Grab a seat, so we can get this show on the road." Born motioned toward the empty chair.

Buda gave the man called Minister one last look before sitting. There was something about him that tugged a familiar cord in his brain. "Did y'all order yet, or were you waiting for me?"

"Just drinks. Me no need no food, because I can't stay long.

Got other business after I leave here," Doodles said in his thick accent.

"Okay, right to business then," Buda replied. "So, we all good for the first shipment?"

"Ya, mon. Me people getting everything ready as we speak," Doodles confirmed. "Delivery soon come, provided that you are still able to handle what we 'bout to drop on you."

"Fo' sho. We ready to rock and roll," Buda assured him.

"Well, that ain't what I hear through the grapevine," Doodles said, much to Buda's surprise.

Buda looked confused. "What the fuck is this nigga talking about?"

"Seems like we have a fly in the ointment," Born told him.

"And what might that be?" Buda asked.

"Eddie," Rolling answered. "He reached out through a friend of a friend and it seems that he ain't as amicable to you moving heroin through his streets."

"*His* streets?" Buda chuckled. "I don't recall him being out there busting his gun when we exterminated Pana and his crew."

"Still, a man like Eddie could present a problem down the road. I thought your boy Diamonds said he worked this shit out with Eddie," Born said.

"He did. I'm sure this is just some type of misunderstanding. I'll take care of it," Buda assured him. Once again Eddie's sneaky ass was stepping on his toes. If he messed up the heroin deal for Buda, it wouldn't matter who his uncle was or how much pull he had. He'd cross that bridge when he came to it.

"Then you best do it quick if you want me drugs," Doodles

said. "Me no want no problems with Eddie or his uncle Michael. Maybe it's best if we hold off until you get this shit straight."

"Wait, but we had a deal!" Buda said.

"No, the deal I make was with Diamonds," Doodles corrected him. "Diamonds, I liked. Him an honorable man, a straightforward man. You, too much double-talk for my taste." He got up from the table.

"Wait a minute, we can work this out." Buda tried to stop him, but Doodles never broke his stride.

"I'll talk to him." T.J. got up and went after him.

"Yo, what the fuck is this shit? You niggas said we was good and now you pull this? I ain't feeling it." Buda slammed his massive fist on the table, drawing the attention of the other diners.

"First of all, lower your muthafucking voice. You talking crazy to me and I'll cut your fucking throat," Rolling hissed. He had dropped his sniveling yes-man persona that he used to fool everyone and had reverted to the cold-blooded mastermind who had coerced Buda to betray his leader at gun-point.

Buda had just finished having a freak session with his girl Mercedes and her girlfriend, Zonnie. He was celebrating their new heroin deal. He found himself surprised when he came out into the living room and found Rolling sitting on the couch between the two ladies—*his* ladies. Rolling Stone had baited a trap and Buda had walked right into it. As it turned out, Doodles had been nothing more than a front man, and Rolling was the plug all along. Rolling could've killed Buda that night if he'd chosen, but instead offered him a deal: usurp Diamonds and take over his position as the distributor of the heroin. Buda wasn't big on the idea of stepping over his childhood friend, but he figured that he didn't have much of a choice. Besides, it was time for some new blood in the crew, a new chief. So he accepted Rolling's bargain and turned a blind eye when Diamonds was taken out.

"Be cool, Rolling." Buda raised his hands in surrender. "We're all friends here, right?"

"Fuck outta here! We ain't friends and will never be friends. You're a means to an end and don't you forget that shit!" Rolling spat.

"Whatever you say, boss," Buda said sarcastically. "By the way, I never got a chance to say thanks for handling that piece of business for me. With Diamonds out of the way the lane is open for me to march my crew into a new era and really get to this money. No more war games."

"Yeah, he's tucked away as snug as a bug in a rug," Born said.

This caught Buda by surprise. "Tucked away? I thought you said Diamonds was going to die."

"And he will, but the when and how ain't our concern. Though by now I'll bet he probably wishes he was." Rolling laughed sinisterly.

Hearing the news that Diamonds was indeed alive made Buda dizzy. Had it not been for the table holding him up he probably would have fallen to the floor. Diamonds was the one person who could dash Buda's plans, and him, straight to hell. "You gotta kill him. Keeping Diamonds alive puts us all at risk," he said nervously.

"If I might interject?" Minister raised his finger. "I can understand your concerns over Diamonds. I've spent time in his company, and I can tell you he's not quite like anyone I've ever met. But at this point he's no longer a threat. My people are seeing to that."

"And who are your people again?" Buda prodded. Minister ignored the question and went back to sipping his water. "Look, y'all don't know Diamonds like I do. So long as there is breath in his body, he's a threat. If you were smart, you'd put him down and be done with it."

"And if you were smart you'd focus on more immediate problems," Rolling countered. "It's time to make a move on my brother."

This made Buda smile. "Sounds good to me. I'll have my people start on the reconnaissance and within a few days we should have his patterns down and figure out the best time to hit him."

"We don't have a few days. This has to go down tonight," Rolling told him.

"Tonight?" Buda shook his head. "Too soon. Big Stone is a careful dude. He keeps no set routine and when he is out and about he's surrounded by shooters. He never lets his guard down."

"Normally everything you're saying is true, but tonight will be different," Rolling said. "My brother is throwing my niece a birthday celebration at his restaurant, but the party is a Trojan horse. While the kids are out front celebrating, my brother will be in the back trying to play United Nations with the power players he feels are still loyal to his cause. A few years ago Big Stone would've never risked bringing those kinds of men in such close proximity to his family. He feels the devil nipping at his heels and he's getting desperate. Desperate men make costly mistakes. Big Stone has unknowingly herded all the cattle into one pen for us to come through and slaughter."

Buda mulled over the information he had just received.

Rolling's conniving ass had laid out one hell of a plan, but there was something he was overlooking. "This shit got the potential to really hit the fan. We knock these old niggas off, their people surely gonna come gunning for us. Knocking off an enemy at a time is one thing, but trying to wipe everybody out at once is an open act of war."

"Can't be no war if everybody has already negotiated terms of surrender. Diamonds saw to that before his untimely retirement." Born smirked.

"What you talking, man?" Buda was confused.

Born looked from Rolling back to Buda. "You mean you didn't know? Me and ya boy Diamonds ain't been cool but a minute, but in that short time I learned something about him: the muthafucka was smart. He understood that you could catch more flies with shit than you could sugar, so *shit* is exactly what he stirred up. Diamonds got into the ears of the disgruntled and under-appreciated number twos and threes, such as myself, and convinced us of a brighter future with us as the new number ones. How do you think he hooked into me?"

"He fixed the fucking fight!" Buda exclaimed, the pieces finally starting to come together.

Rolling clapped his hands. "Give the smart kid a cookie. Diamonds laid out the perfect plan, and had he stuck to the script I'd be about to open up the heroin pipeline instead of you. The moment I caught wind of him catching feelings for my niece I knew he had become a liability, and couldn't risk him not doing what needed to be done when we moved to take my brother out. This is why he had to be replaced."

For a long while all Buda could do was sit there dumbfounded.

Diamonds was a man who always kept an extra ace up his sleeve, and this situation proved it. The things that troubled him were: How did Rolling and Born seem to know more about Diamonds' master plan than his second in command? If the New Yorkers knew, it was possible that members of Diamonds' crew had been aware too. Was Buda the odd man out? Suddenly he didn't feel as in control as he thought when he'd first taken up the mantle of chief.

"So, what's up, Buda? Your people gonna do this or what? We may not get another shot cleaner than this one," Born said.

"Yeah, it'll take some doing, but we'll make it happen," Buda told him. "But listen, if we do this then I'm going to need something for me."

"Giving you everything that was promised to Diamonds isn't enough?" Rolling asked.

Buda shrugged. "We'll call this the icing on the cake. The minute I lay your brother out, you have to lay mine. Diamonds has to die."

"Buda, I keep trying to tell you that I no longer speak for Diamonds' life," Rolling reaffirmed.

"Then you need to get word to whoever does," Buda shot back. "My hold on the crew will never be absolute so long as he lives."

Rolling cast a glance at Minister, whose face remained neutral. "How about we revisit this conversation when my brother is off the throne and I'm on it?"

"Then our business here is concluded." Buda stood up from the table. "Call me later on with the time and the place and your brother is a done deal."

"You do realize Big Slim is never going to sign off on you killing Diamonds to appease Buda," Minister said after Buda had gone. "His beef with Diamonds goes back too far and cuts too deep for anyone to have that pleasure but him."

"Of course I know that. I've found that empty promises keep dumb-ass niggas like him motivated." Rolling laughed. "You know I can't help but wonder what Buda would think if he knew the heroin we're going to be hitting his crew with is being imported from the man they ripped off to start building Diamonds' empire, Big Slim."

"You know what they say: everything comes full cipher." Born painted an imaginary circle with his finger.

"So you think they'll really be able to pull this off?" Rolling asked Born.

"I'm pretty sure of it. Even without Diamonds leading them they're still the hungriest pack of dogs I've ever seen."

"Something I still don't get," Minister interjected. "If Buda and Diamonds were supposed to be tight, what would make him stab him in the back like this?"

Rolling's voice was icy when he answered, "Sometimes you get tired of waiting your turn."

PART

SAINTS & SINNERS

CHAPTER FIFTEEN

"Can I ask you something?" Power asked from the passenger seat of Knowledge's car. They had ben riding around for the last two hours trying to get a lead on the bandits who had killed Oscar and Pat.

"Sure, what up?" Knowledge changed lanes without signaling. They were heading south on Lenox Avenue.

"When are you gonna retire this shit?" Power asked, speaking of Knowledge's car. It was a 1993 booger-green Acura Legend that appeared to be on its last legs.

"Ain't shit wrong with my car," Knowledge said defensively.

"Ain't shit right with it either! Homie, you riding around in this got Big Stone looking bad, like he don't take care of his people," Power joked.

"See, that's the difference between me and you. I don't care about other people's opinions," Knowledge told him.

"Well, you should. One day you're probably gonna be running this whole shit and appearances are important. At least pull out your Range once in a while." Power was speaking of the truck

Knowledge had purchased a year prior. It was a 2005 fully loaded Range Rover. He had spent a grip on it, but hardly drove it.

"And have every eye in the hood on me? No thanks."

"Then what'd you drop all that bread on it for if you ain't gonna show it off?" Power asked.

"Because I can," Knowledge told him flatly. In Knowledge's position the ability to move unseen was one of his greatest assets, which is why he chose to spend most of his time driving the clunker. The Acura was an unremarkable vehicle that didn't warrant a second look, so by the time anyone noticed him it was already too late. The only reason he had even purchased the Range Rover is because Big Stone had pressured him into it. Much like Power, he was always on Knowledge's back about appearances and perception.

"So, you make any progress on finding these guys yet?" Power asked.

"Not a whole lot, and Big Stone is on my ass about it. In all the years I've been working for him this is the first time I can ever remember seeing him this rattled."

"I can't say that I blame him, man. The whole city is buzzing about these dudes and the shit they been putting down. Everybody is on edge thinking they're next."

"Yeah, all that chatter and not one solid fucking lead as to who they are." Knowledge was frustrated. His inability to track down the bandits who were hunting New York bosses was beginning to make him question himself.

"Don't be too hard on yourself, Knowledge. These dudes are slippery as hell, but we'll find them," Power assured his friend.

"*We?*" Knowledge gave him a questioning look. "Power, I appreciate you standing in for me and babysitting Pearl for a few hours, but I ain't trying to pull you back into this shit. Especially after all you had to do to get out."

Power and Knowledge had been running the streets together since they were kids. A few years prior they had gotten caught up in a sting. They were both looking at time, but Power knew Knowledge was on Big Stone's radar and being groomed for great things, while he had nothing and no one. Power ate the charges so that Knowledge could go free. After doing his time, Power turned his life around and went straight. He had a steady job cutting hair at the barbershop and sold a little weed on the side for extra money, but outside of that he wasn't in the game anymore.

"Dawg, I told you when you came to see me the other day that the only thing that could bring me out of retirement is a nigga trying to hurt you, and that's exactly what these muthafuckas are trying to do. I can go back to cutting hair when this shit is over, but right now I got my brother's back." Power held out his fist.

"Solid." Knowledge gave him dap. If there was no one else in the world he could depend on, he knew Power would always be in his corner. He took comfort in having his partner back with him.

They ended up getting caught at a red light on 145th and Lenox. Knowledge drummed his fingers impatiently on the wheel, waiting for it to change. As he was checking out the scenery his eyes drifted to the gaping hole that had once been Pops's bar. The fire had destroyed the place, leaving nothing in its wake but memories of the landmark. Knowledge had had some good times in that bar and he was sorry to hear that it was gone. Looking at it also reminded him of the last conversation he'd had with Pearl on that corner.

It had been the same day they found out two of her friends were caught in the fire, and they had taken Pearl to the hospital to visit with Marissa, the friend who survived, while Big Stone and Knowledge were on another floor giving Pops the third degree. Pearl had taken the news of her friend dying pretty hard and had run off. Of course it had been up to Knowledge to track her down. He found her at the remains of the bar, talking to a dude whom Knowledge had seen before in passing. He was a country-sounding dude with long dreads and jeweled teeth. Knowledge had learned from Pearl that his name was Diamonds. She claimed that he was an old friend, but from the way Diamonds was recklessly eyeballing Knowledge over Pearl it had felt as if there was more to it than that. Thankfully their brief confrontation ended without violence, but something about the man had been nagging at Knowledge ever since. It hadn't dawned on Knowledge at the time, but Diamonds fit a loose description that had been given by a homeless man who had witnessed Pana's execution. *Teeth that sparkled like glass,* had been his exact words. Knowledge had been hoping to cross paths with Diamonds again, but he hadn't seen a trace of him since. He'd considered asking Pearl about him, but didn't want to raise suspicions.

"Yo, the name Diamonds mean anything to you?" Knowledge asked Power.

Power thought on it. "Doesn't ring a bell. Is he somebody I should know?"

"Nah, I just asked because I know a lot of information passes through that barbershop you cut hair in. He's some nobody nigga who I caught pushing up on Pearl, but something about the boy don't feel right."

"I always say trust your gut. If he don't feel right then he probably isn't. You think he's tied up in this shit?" Power asked.

"I won't know for sure until I do some more digging. Just the same, keep your ear to the street for me."

"You got that. So, where we off to now?"

"To follow up on the only real lead I've had since this shit started." Knowledge went on to tell him about the horn-playing girl who had been a part of Oscar's murder.

"A bitch playing a trumpet? That ain't something you see every day in New York," Power pointed out.

"I know, which is why I'm hoping that makes it easier to narrow it down."

"Any ideas on where we should start looking for this chick?"

"Not yet, but I know who can put us on the right track. Only one dude I know in the city who makes his coin off being able to read women's minds."

Power gave him a disbelieving look. "God, I know you ain't suggesting we go see that powder puff? Come on, man, you know he makes me uncomfortable. I don't like the way he looks at me."

"Well, you can wait in the car. I need to see this dude. If anybody knows this chick, it's him. Or at the very least he can put us in contact with somebody who does."

"If you say so, I'm with you, but the sun is still up and you know nobody sees him until sundown, like he's some kind of freaking vampire. What makes you think he'll be willing to break his rule to meet with you?"

Knowledge reached into the glove compartment and pulled out an envelope. "Because I come bearing gifts."

Hades was quickly becoming one of Spanish Harlem's best-kept secrets. It was an after-hours spot where you could get a cheap drink as well as indulge in illicit vices. You wouldn't know it, though, because it was well hidden. It was one of those places that everyone talked about but no one, other than those who had been inside, could verify its existence. Knowledge had been there once, but quickly found that he didn't have the taste or the stomach for the things that went on there. Had he not been so desperate to get a lead on the girl with the horn he would've just as soon avoided the place altogether.

"You coming inside?" Knowledge asked Power, once he had parked the car.

Power peered out the window at the spot. "Not unless you need me to watch your back?"

"Probably not. These dudes are pretty tame unless pushed, so I should be good." Knowledge got out of the car.

Knowledge's entrance was announced by the ringing of the tiny bell that hung over the front door. There was an old man behind the counter, shoveling a loaf of dough into the oven. The reason Hades was so hard to find was because it was an actual functioning bakery. People came in and out of there all day long getting fresh-baked bread and pastries, but had they known what Knowledge knew they would've thought twice about eating anything that came out of those ovens. Bread wasn't the only thing they baked in Hades.

Knowledge stopped and nodded to the old man in greeting.

"In the back," the old man responded. Knowledge had called ahead, so they were expecting him.

He passed through double doors that led him into the storeroom. There were boxes lining the shelves marked FLOUR, SUGAR, and for other baking ingredients but Knowledge doubted half the labels depicted what was actually in the boxes. The man he had come to see was a dabbler in all things, but pussy and pills were his cash cows. When he reached the door at the other end of the storeroom, Knowledge's nose picked up on the faintest traces of liquor and sex, likely still lingering from the night before. He had just raised his hand to knock on the door when it swung open and he was confronted with something that made him cringe.

It wasn't Knowledge's first time meeting the doorman/bodyguard, but no matter how many times he saw him he could never get used to his appearance. He stood about six-foot-seven and was built like a truck. His large block head bobbled on his shoulders as if it were too heavy for his neck. A scar shaped like a lightning bolt stretched from his flat forehead and stopped just above his droopy eye. He bore a striking resemblance to Frankenstein, which is how he had acquired his nickname.

"Frank," Knowledge greeted him with a curt nod.

"Sup, Knowledge?" Frank replied in a voice that sounded like an old car engine trying to turn over.

"Your boss is expecting me."

"Yeah, he said you'd be coming by. He's getting himself together and said I should let you in to wait." Frank pushed the door open for Knowledge to pass through it. "If you need anything, I'll be right outside," he said, closing the door behind him.

They called the room an office, but it was little more than a wooden table, some chairs, and a file cabinet. Knowledge doubted that anything aside from bakery business went on in there. The fact that he was received in the office told Knowledge that his host was leery of his intentions. Knowledge would expect nothing less from a man who moved like he did. He was a friend to no one except those in his immediate circle.

Knowledge didn't have to wait long before the door opened again and his host finally showed himself. He was a tall, athletically built man with smooth caramel skin and girlish lips. He was shirtless under his gold kimono and matching pajama pants. His processed hair was wrapped in a silk head scarf that was tied to the front Aunt Jemima–style. Pinched between his freshly manicured fingers was a thin joint off of which he took slow drags. Despite his less than masculine appearance, Christian Knight was a man you did not want to end up on the wrong side of.

"Well, this is a welcome surprise." Christian smiled like the cat who had just swallowed the canary. His dark eyes drank Knowledge in.

"Thanks for agreeing to see me. I know these ain't your normal business hours," Knowledge told him.

Christian waved him off. "How could I refuse an emissary of Big Stone? Besides, I was curious as to why you asked for this meeting. You don't do drugs, aside from weed, and you don't buy pussy. So what business could we possibly have?"

"I'm in need of some information."

Christian looked disappointed. "And here I thought you had come to hand-deliver an invitation to that big party your boss is throwing tonight, because I sure didn't get one in the mail," he said sarcastically.

"You know that wasn't my call. I had no say over who got invited. I'm just a hired gun," Knowledge said, downplaying his position.

Christian sat on the edge of the table in front of Knowledge. "Come on, you don't have to play coy with me. Everyone knows you're the heir apparent to the Kingdom of Stone. But that's a conversation for another time. What kind of information is it that you need and what are you willing to pay for it? You know nothing in Hades is free."

"Of course not." Knowledge pulled out the envelope. "A few months back you had an incident with one of your girls. A john cut her face up pretty bad."

"Cassie." Christian nodded, remembering the pretty little white girl who had made him so much money. "That girl needed four surgeries on her face after what he did. She'll never be the same again," he said angrily. "He's lucky the police got to him before I did. I've spread a few dollars around throughout the prisons, but so far haven't been able to turn up shit on him."

"That's because he ain't locked up. He snitched on some dudes he was getting money with so the police cut him a deal. They gave him a new name and a new address, both of which are in this envelope." Christian reached for it, but Knowledge held it just outside his reach. "Information first, address after."

"Fair enough," Christian agreed. "What do you need to know?"

"I need some information on a chick. Slim broad, kinda cute, and known to play a trumpet. She's probably working with a crew of dudes, likely out-of-towners."

Christian tapped one of his gold-painted nails on his chin while he thought about it. "I'm sorry, but it doesn't ring a bell."

"Come on, Christian. You got your fingers in the pussies and this one don't sound familiar?" Knowledge pressed.

Christian laughed. "Trust me, if I did have a line on her, she'd be working in one of my spots. A pretty girl who is musically gifted could fetch me a nice piece of change. You'd be surprised at the fetishes some of my clients have. Why are you looking for her anyway? She trying to pin a baby on you or something?"

"Nah, nothing like that. I think she may be connected to all these bodies that have been dropping lately."

"Yes, I've been hearing about that. Nasty thing; the cocaine business, that is. That's why I keep it to pills and pussy. Happy people are less likely to wanna blow your head off over some bullshit," Christian said.

"You're right about that," Knowledge agreed. "Well, if you hear anything, let me know." He handed him the envelope and stood to leave.

"You still gonna give me this even though I couldn't help you find this girl?" Christian was surprised.

Knowledge shrugged. "Think of it as a down payment on the next favor I may have to come in here to ask. Thanks for your time." He was about to walk out when Christian stopped him.

"You said this girl is likely working with a crew from out of town?"

"Yeah, why? You know something?" Knowledge asked hopefully.

"Maybe, but I'm not too sure if the two are connected. A few nights ago we had to toss some country nigga out on his ass. He was all in his feelings over one of our girls, Mercedes. She was on the clock with another trick and it didn't seem to sit too well with him."

"What happened to this dude after y'all tossed him?" Knowledge asked.

"The police took his uncouth ass to jail. I was going to send Frankie and Boogie down there to let him know how much I didn't appreciate him causing trouble in my spot, but he had already been released. Apparently, he was plugged in with a local dick-head detective in the department so the charges magically disappeared." Christian twinkled his fingers like he was casting a spell.

"Would you happen to know this detective's name?"

"Knowledge, baby, that's a tree I don't think you wanna climb. This dude is more gangster than police," Christian warned.

"This detective may be the best chance I got at tracking this crew down and stopping them."

"Frankly, that ain't my problem. I'm sorry for the losses you guys are taking, but me and mine are on go all day, every day. Anybody come trying to take a piece of this sweet ass is going to have a problem I seriously doubt they want," Christian boasted.

"I'm sure that's the same thing Pana Suarez said before they cut his heart out and murdered his entire crew."

This seemed to get Christian's attention. He and Pana weren't friends, but Pana's crew had done a few jobs for him. Christian knew how the man rolled, so when heard that he had gotten hit, he knew whoever had done it was about their business. Pana's crew was strong, but Christian knew if the bandits were able to take down Pana, he himself didn't have a snowball's chance in hell if they ever turned their attention to his business.

"Knowledge, if I give you this name you didn't hear it from me. The last thing I want is that crazy-ass cop sniffing around my shit. Are we clear on that?"

"That goes without saying. I just wanna have a chat with him," Knowledge assured him.

"Well, you do so at your own peril. His name is Detective James Wolf, but they call him the Lone Wolf because of the high mortality rate of every partner he's ever had. You can ask any knucklehead on the streets about him because at one time or another he's either had his hand in their pockets or his foot in their asses."

Knowledge had heard the name on the streets. Wolf was like the boogeyman to dope boys throughout Harlem. His attachment to suspect cases was only preceded by his attachment to unsavory characters throughout the underworld. Wolf was as dirty as shit-kickers boots, but no one had been able to successfully pin anything on him. Likely because most witnesses to his dirt never lived to take the stand against him. Knowledge had once dropped an envelope off to the detective on behalf of Big Stone, so he was familiar with the watering hole he hung around. Wolf shouldn't prove too hard to track down, but finding the detective was one thing, getting him to talk was something else.

"Thanks, Christian."

"My pleasure, handsome." Christian stubbed his joint out in the ashtray. "Why don't you drop in one of these nights and party at Hades. Let me and some of my girls show you how the other half lives."

"Thanks, but I've already seen that movie and I'm not a fan. Later, Christian."

"So how was your chat with *el príncipe de la noche*?" Power asked when Knowledge was back in the car. It translated to Prince of the Night, which is what some called Christian.

"Enlightening," Knowledge said, starting the car.

"So, where to now?"

Knowledge looked at his watch. "I've got a little bit of time to kill before I have to go home and get ready for tonight. I got one more tree to shake. Let's go see a man about a dog."

CHAPTER SIXTEEN

After getting out of Buda's car, Vita took a taxi farther south to get hers. She had left it near the diner on Broadway where they had all met up before the hit on Oscar.

She was still pissed about the way Buda had come at her, but she didn't know why she was surprised. Buda had always been envious of Diamonds and probably couldn't wait until he was out of the way so he could help himself to everything Diamonds had once laid claim to, including Vita. And to think she had almost bought that corny-ass story about him secretly being sweet on her. She wouldn't let him into her pants if his was the last dick on earth.

Thinking of dick turned her attention to Domo. He'd seemed troubled about something when last she'd seen him. It's possible that he was still sore over Buda pulling a gun on him, but she doubted it. Domo was too tough to let something like that crawl under his skin. If she had to bet she'd say it was the exchange they'd had that morning. Domo had accused her of forcing him to compete with a ghost, and though she had denied it at the time she knew he was right. Vita would always love Diamonds, that would never change, but the more time she spent with Domo the easier it was becoming to let go of what she'd had with Diamonds. What was troubling Vita was his abrupt departure. It didn't feel right, like she was overlooking something. Which is what now brought her to his apartment building.

In the other cities they had laid siege to, the crew had always bunked under the same roof, but that had changed when they arrived in New York. Diamonds was renting a nice three-bedroom apartment in an upscale Manhattan neighborhood that overlooked Central Park. He'd gotten into the building through a crooked member of the management. They allowed him to make a no-questions-asked cash payment so long as he took out a five-year lease and greased their palms for the hookup.

Vita pulled into the underground garage and began trying to retrace Diamonds' steps. If she could get into his head then she might be able to get a better idea of what had happened to him. Much to her surprise his SUV was in its normal parking spot. This told her that he had at least made it home. She tried the doors, but they were locked. She peered through the window and spotted a purse on the floor in the back. It was a high-end-looking bag, out of the price range of the hood rats Diamonds chose to cat around with, but it did look like something his new friend Pearl would carry. Knowing Pearl had been the last one to see Diamonds made Vita wonder if there was something to Buda's theory about Pearl's father being involved in the disappearance. It made her sick to see him fawning over her at the baby shower, but she held her tongue to keep the peace.

She walked through the dimly lit garage, blowing bubbles with the gum she was chewing, eyes scanning for additional clues. Her path led her to the elevator to the lobby and the apartments above. The doors slid open and she startled an unsuspecting elderly white couple who were getting off. The husband clutched his wife tightly as they slid past Vita. She lowered her head, trying to hide the smirk that had broken out across her face. It was then that something caught her eye. She stopped the door from closing and peered through the small crack at the base of the elevator. It was dark and the shaft was littered with trash, but she thought she saw what looked like a cell phone.

Vita got down on one knee and tried to slide her fingers in the crack, but it was too narrow. This would require a bit of resourcefulness on her part. She removed the necklace she was wearing and placed her gum on the end of it. It would be a long shot, but short of trying to get the building maintenance staff to shut the elevator down it was the only play she had. It took her five attempts before she was finally able to get the gum to hold firm enough to move the cell phone. Vita focused with the steadiness of a bomb specialist while pulling the cell phone up. If she dropped it she seriously doubted she'd get the gum to stick a second time. After holding her breath for what seemed like an eternity, she managed to retrieve the cell phone. She had been right, it was Diamonds'! It was completely dead from sitting for so long, but it was the first solid lead she'd had since his disappearance. She would take it up to his apartment to charge it and prayed to God it yielded something to go on rather than another dead end.

Vita let herself into Diamonds' apartment with the spare key he had given her. Goldie and Vita were the only ones he'd trusted enough to have one. When she entered the apartment she immediately felt a chill run over her shoulders. A quick examination of the doorframe revealed etchings in the paint so faint you'd likely never notice them unless someone told you to look. They were the same markings Diamonds used over the entrance of every place they had ever laid their heads. He told them it was to keep the evil out. She had never put much stock in Diamonds' superstitious practices, more from not *wanting* to believe them than actually *not* believing. She had been around Diamonds long enough to know that he was involved in things that couldn't be explained by modern science.

The first thing she did was go to the kitchen, where she knew Diamonds always kept his phone charger plugged over the microwave. She waited on pins and needles while the phone absorbed enough juice to power on and then began her search. He'd had several missed calls, mostly from her and Goldie, and even a few from Hank. The rest of the numbers she didn't recognize, but what she did notice was that Buda's number was absent from the call log. This just confirmed what she had already suspected, that he was the least concerned about Diamonds' disappearance.

While going through Diamonds' texts she finally broke luck. *Don't go home until we talk,* the message read. It was from someone listed as the Howling, which she knew was a fake name for his contact in the police department, Detective Wolf. She had met with him several times with Diamonds. Why didn't the detective want Diamonds to go home and how did it tie into his disappearance? She planned to ask the detective in person the minute she left the apartment.

Finding nothing else of note, Vita moved to the bedroom. As messy as Diamonds could be with the hearts of women, the same couldn't be said about his treatment of his bedroom. All his clothes were on hangers and the shoes stacked in neat boxes. His bed was still perfectly made, with the corners of the blanket tucked in military-style so she knew it hadn't been slept in. At least Pearl hadn't made it that far. Vita sat on the edge of the bed and ran her hand over the surface of the blanket. At one time she had known every inch of it intimately, but now it felt alien. She picked up one of his pillows and inhaled deeply. It still smelled of Diamonds, but there was something else too . . . burning sage. She sniffed the air and realized it wasn't coming from the pillow, but somewhere else in the apartment. She wasn't alone.

Pistol in hand, Vita crept through the apartment looking for the source of the scent. It was strongest outside the spare room that Diamonds sometimes used as an office. The door was partially open and she could hear what sounded like someone speaking in a hushed tone. Whoever had violated her former lover's safe haven would pay for the offense in blood. Using the barrel of the gun she pushed the door wider and was surprised to find Goldie inside.

Diamonds' baby brother was hunched over a card table, rocking back and forth and speaking in tongues. His fist was balled and held above the table, moving in a counterclockwise circle. Sage burned in a bowl, and next to it sat a bloody knife.

"Goldie?" Vita called out softly. If he knew she was standing there he showed no signs of it. "Goldie, baby, what you doing?" She moved in closer. It was then that she noticed the blood dripping from his hand onto the table. "Oh my goodness!" She rushed to his side. When she touched him, she noticed his skin was on fire. "Goldie, Goldie!" She called his name over and over while shaking him. When he was still unresponsive she slapped him across the face to break him out of his trance.

"D'fuck!" Goldie recoiled. He blinked twice as if he was trying to figure out who Vita was. For a minute it looked like he was about to reach for the bloodied knife that lay on the table beside him.

"Goldie, it's me!" she announced herself.

"Vita?" The fog began to roll back from his brain.

"Boy, what in the hell are you in here doing to yourself?" Vita picked up his bloody hand to examine it. Thankfully it was only a flesh wound.

"This!" Goldie slammed his fist onto the table, smearing blood over what appeared to be a map of New York. "I watched Auntie and Diamonds work this trick at least a half dozen times, but it ain't working for me. I probably need to offer more blood." He reached for the knife, but Vita snatched it away.

"The last thing you need is to bleed any more. You know better than to be in here trafficking in them black things," Vita scolded him while looking over the bloody map. "What are you doing anyway?"

"Long time ago, when we was kids still living out in the bayou, Auntie taught us about the blood tether," Goldie began. "She say that me and my brother tethered by blood and spirit. If ever we should get separated then the blood would call to blood. It's how we were able to find him when he was caught up in that foolishness with the old witch Bleu. The blood led us right to the shack where they were holding my brother."

"So why isn't it working now?" Vita asked.

"I got no idea." Goldie shrugged. "I been in here trying to get it right, but it keeps taking me to this spot." He tapped an area on the map marked Upper Bay. "So either my brother sprouted gills and turned into a fish, or this spell is busted."

"We can figure it out later. Right now I need to get you cleaned up so we can follow up on a lead I found in Diamonds' cell phone."

"Where'd you find my brother's jack?"

"I'll explain later. Now go wash that blood off you." Vita shooed him. While Goldie was in the bathroom washing up, Vita took a second look at the map. He had made a mess of it by bleeding all over the thing. She followed the trickle; just as Goldie had pointed out it seemed to stop in the middle of a body of water marked Upper Bay, between Red Hook in Brooklyn and Bayonne, New Jersey. As she looked closer she noticed something obscured by one of the drops. Using her thumb she wiped the blood away and uncovered a speck of land. "Liberty Island," she read aloud. That's where the Statue of Liberty was located. She knew this because it was one of the first places she had Diamonds take her to visit when they had first arrived in New York. She had been fascinated with it since she had first read about it in school. They spent the day exploring as much of the place as they could, even managing to sneak into a section at the northern end that was closed to the public due to renovations that were under way. It had been fairly simple to do; it was isolated and the only part of the island that wasn't teeming with security.

Before Vita could ponder her discovery further, Goldie came out of the bathroom. He was talking on his cell phone and his expression was grim. "A'ight. We'll be right there," he said and ended the call.

"Everything good?" she asked.

"That was the nigga Buda."

"Fuck did he want?" Vita asked in a sour tone.

"He says he got the official word that it was Big Stone who gave the order on Diamonds, so we got the green light to move on him. Tonight we hunting *big* game."

This surprised Vita. "What the fuck? He know we always track our marks at least twenty-four hours. What's with all this spontaneous shit lately?"

Goldie shrugged. "I don't know, and truthfully I don't care. Only thing I'm worried about is putting a hole in the nigga who laid hands on my brother. Oh, and he said to bring your little boyfriend too. This is an all-hands-on deck situation."

An uneasy feeling settled in the pit of Vita's stomach. Buda was moving way too fast for her liking. Also troubling was his insistence that Domo be there. She had yet to tell Domo that she was aware of his connection to the family they were about to move on, and right before wiping them out wasn't how she pictured breaking the news to him. How would he react when he found out the man they were about to assassinate was one of his best friend's father?

"About that lead you said you found; how solid is it?" Goldie asked.

"Solid enough for us to put Buda's fat ass on hold for a few while we check it out."

CHAPTER SEVENTEEN

Hank was relieved when the last of the packages had been wrapped up and he was able to leave Mousey's house. Between Willie and Lucky's back-and-forth arguing and Mousey's constant begging for a hit he felt like he was about to snap. He wasn't sure if it was old age or trying to adapt to a city as big as New York, but the game was losing its luster for him. This was why he had started stacking his paper to eventually retire. In Hank's time on earth he had put a lot of mileage on his body. From being rich to becoming a fiend to being shot and doing stints in various prisons, he had seen his fair share of highs and lows, and thankfully was still around to reflect on them. In fact, the only reason he probably still played the game was on the strength of Diamonds.

Thinking of Diamonds brought a deep sadness over Hank. He had known him since he was a small child, barefoot and stealing for his meals. Even as a youth Hank had seen the larceny lurking in the young man's heart and he fed it. It was Hank who had first turned Diamonds on to selling drugs, by having him hustle weed out of his grocery store. Diamonds had always been a good hustler, but Hank had watched him grow into something more and he wasn't sure if he was proud or afraid for him. In a sense Hank felt responsible for putting Diamonds on the corrupt path and the guilt of this is what really kept him close.

Hank had been replaying his last days with Diamonds over in his head and couldn't understand how he hadn't seen it coming. His one-time ward had always been reckless, but more so when he started to rise to power. Diamonds had been running around like he was invincible, and the one person who was supposed to step up and check him didn't, and now they were stuck with that idiot Buda as their chief. When Buda had invited Hank to challenge him for the position, he almost accepted but thought better of it. Hank's time had come and gone. It was a young man's game to play now. Besides, he had seen what happened to those who wore the crown. No matter how good their hearts were the power always eventually corrupted them. Diamonds had been a perfect example of that. Someone who had so much promise that couldn't seem to get out of his own way. Hank prayed to whatever God would listen that Diamonds was still alive out there somewhere, but if he wasn't at least he was free now.

After leaving the Bronx he headed out to Queens, where he was to meet his lady friend, Elaine, and grab a bite to eat. They had met by chance one day when Hank was in Harlem doing some shopping on 125th Street. He was trying to decide on a pair of sneakers to buy, but found himself clueless. Hank had always fancied himself a Stacy Adams man, so picking out running shoes was out of his depth. Elaine had taken mercy on the confused man and helped him out with his purchase. She was younger than he, but had her shit together. Elaine owned her own car, home, and a thriving salon called Rouge. This is why they were meeting all the way in Queens because she was out there looking at a storefront where she was thinking of opening a second location. Hank admired Elaine for her ambition, as well as the things she could do in the bedroom.

Their rendezvous was at a diner a few blocks from where Elaine was viewing the property. When Hank arrived, she was already seated. She was a light-skinned woman, just shy of forty, with curves in all the right places. Hank loved it when she wore tight clothes because she filled them out so well, but that afternoon she was looking professional in a business suit and pumps. When she saw him walk in she stood to greet him.

"Hey you!" Elaine kissed him once on each cheek. "Thanks for coming out all this way to eat with me."

"Wasn't 'bout nothing. You know I'd drive a million miles to spend a few minutes in your company."

"Listen to you on your Billy Dee," she teased.

"So, how'd things go with the storefront?"

"It actually went pretty well. I looked at three properties, but I think I've settled on one I like. It's huge and the rent is cheap."

"A lot of space for cheap rent in New York must mean something is wrong with it," Hank joked.

"Let's hope not." Elaine crossed herself. "I really wanna get this second location up an running. But enough about me. How was your day?"

Hank shrugged. "Same as any other I gather. Just had to handle some family business."

"Ah, the family again. And when do you plan to stop hiding

me from your family? You talk about them all the time, but we've been dating for months and I still haven't met them."

"Soon, baby," Hank promised. Elaine was the only part of his life that his crew didn't have access to. She was his solitude and he wanted to keep it that way for as long as he could. "Did you order yet?" he changed the subject.

Hank and Elaine sat chatting over two fish dinners, making small talk about love, life, and everything between. He loved talking to Elaine because she was smart and ambitious. It made him feel good to be around her.

Halfway through their meal Hank spotted a buxom Puerto Rican girl walk in. The sun hadn't even fully set yet, so at that hour of the day dressed in a short skirt and high boots she looked like she was either getting ready for the club or the track. He guessed the latter. As he continued to watch her he realized that he knew her . . . well, he had at least seen her before. It was Mercedes, one of Buda's broads. She was the only girl Hank had ever seen stretch Buda's nose open wider than the Holland Tunnel. Buda was so sprung on her that he wouldn't even bring her around the crew, as if he were afraid one of them would try and poach on her.

Mercedes walked across the diner and stopped at a table where a couple were sitting: a pretty light-skinned girl with a blond weave and a gentleman dressed in a white turtleneck and blazer. Hank had to blink twice to make sure his eyes weren't playing tricks on him. He almost hadn't recognized the man, without his baggy clothes and those god-awful do-rags he loved to wear, but it was Born's partner, Rolling Stone. What the hell was he doing talking with Buda's girl and why was he dressed like that? The plot thickened when Mercedes leaned in and kissed Rolling Stone on the lips and then kissed the blonde. Hank continued to watch as they exchanged a few pleasant words before Rolling dropped some bills on the table and the three of them walked out together. What the hell was going on?

"See something you like?" Elaine asked with an attitude.

"Nah, it ain't like that. I think I know that dude. Gimme a second." Hank excused himself and hurried out the front door but by the time he made it outside there was no sign of the trio.

After they had finished eating, Hank walked Elaine back to her car. She tried to get him to come by her place, but he took a rain check. His mind was still stuck on Rolling and the two girls. Something was amiss and he needed to find out what.

He saw Elaine off before walking to his own car, which was parked on a side block two streets over. He was fumbling in his pocket for his keys when he felt someone behind him. He turned and was surprised to see Rolling standing there.

"Damn, you scared the shit out of me."

"Sorry about that. I saw you back at the diner. I was gonna walk my ladies to the taxi and come back to see what was up with you, but you were already gone," Rolling told him. "So who was that you were sitting with? That your girl?"

"Nah, just some bitch I met this morning and was trying to fuck," Hank lied. Something about the way Rolling was looking at him sent a warning bell ringing in his head. "What's up with the outfit? You going to a funeral or something?"

"Actually, yes. Yours." Rolling produced a pistol and shot Hank in the gut.

Hank slid down the side of his car, eyes looking up at Rolling in total shock.

"Try not to take this personal, Hank. I actually liked you. You just picked the wrong diner to eat in today." Rolling leveled his gun. As Hank laid there, fighting to breathe, he croaked out, "Why?"

"Because I'm not ready for the other shoe to drop jus' yet," Rolling told him before pulling the trigger three more times.

CHAPTER EIGHTEEN

It took Knowledge a little longer than expected to track down the elusive detective. Wolf spent his nights trolling the streets of New York like some dark avenger, but he spent his days getting shit-faced in one of three watering holes that he was partial to. Knowledge and Power had visited two already with no luck, but hoped that would change with the third: a spot called Midian.

"What the fuck would a cop be doing hanging out in this joint?" Power asked, looking at the spot.

"Your guess is as good as mine. I ain't here to judge the man, just ask a few questions," Knowledge said. "Wait for me by the car, this shouldn't take but a few minutes."

"Nah, God. I don't like the looks of this place."

"Me either, but I don't wanna spook this dude by rolling in deep. He's kinda skittish and I don't want him to buck unnecessarily."

"A'ight, it's your call," Power relented and went to sit on the hood of the car. He hated waiting on the sidelines, but he trusted Knowledge's judgment.

When Knowledge stepped into the bar all eyes seemed to turn to him. He imagined he stuck out like a sore thumb, dressed in jeans and Timberlands in a room full of men and women wearing mostly leather and denim. Midian was a biker bar located in a rough section of Hell's Kitchen and off limits to the faint of heart.

Knowledge scanned the faces of the few people inside drinking, but saw no sign of Wolf. He crossed the room and found an empty stool at the end of the bar, near a table where two men were playing pool. That vantage point gave him a clear view of the door so he could see anyone coming or going before they saw him.

"You sure you in the right place?" The bartender had appeared as if by magic. She was a gray-haired hag, with tattoos covering her arms and neck beneath a leather corset that did its best to hold up her sagging breasts.

"Pretty sure," Knowledge replied. "I'll have a Howl at the Moon," he said, repeating the code words he'd used when Big Stone had last sent him to drop something to the detective.

The hag narrowed her eyes at him. "Never heard of Howl at the Moon. We only serve beer and whisky here."

"A beer, then."

The bartender gave him one last distrustful look before heading down to the other end of the bar where the beer coolers were. She came back a few seconds later and slammed the beer on the counter in front of him. "Five bucks."

Knowledge handed her a twenty. "Keep the change."

The bartender held the bill up to the light to make sure it was real before stuffing it into her corset and walking off.

For the next half hour or so Knowledge sipped his beer, watching the bar. Every time someone entered, he looked up hopefully but so far there had been no sign of the detective. He had begun to think that it was a dead end, until he spotted a couple stroll into the bar. The man was tall, wearing a baseball cap pulled low on his head. A black bandanna was tied snugly around his neck. He was an unsavory-looking character, but Knowledge was more focused on the girl with him. Her wig was a different color than the first time their paths had crossed, but Knowledge would recognize that walk anywhere. She moved with a swagger that was unmistakable. It was the same girl who had been in Pops's hospital room the day he and Big Stone had visited him.

"Fuck we doing way down here, V?" Goldie looked at the front of the rundown bar in disgust.

"This is where he wants to meet," Vita told him. After several frustrating attempts she had managed to finally get hold of Detective Wolf. He wouldn't answer when she tried to call from her phone, but picked up when she called from Diamonds' cell. He seemed surprised to hear it was Vita on the other end. In their brief conversation he told her that he had information about what he thought may have happened to Diamonds, but wouldn't talk about it on the phone. So they'd arranged a face-to-face meeting at a spot called Midian.

"Well, I hope this nigga has news about my brother, because if he doesn't he's gonna regret wasting my fucking time," Goldie said in frustration.

"Easy, bruh. Wolf ain't your average police. We gotta handle this situation with kid gloves, so best you let me do the talking," Vita cautioned before leading the way inside the bar. She strutted into the joint like she owned the place, turning quite a few heads as she crossed the room to the bar. Behind it was an old tattooed crone, wiping out a glass with a greasy rag. She gave Vita a look that said her kind wasn't welcome there, but Vita didn't care. "Two Howl at the Moons," she ordered.

"You're the second person to ask for one of those today, and I'm going to tell you like I told them: we don't serve those here," the old woman said in a nasty tone.

"C'mon, sis. Why are you acting like you've never seen me in here before? You know what I want," Vita insisted.

The old woman shrugged. "I see a lot of coloreds in here lately. What makes you so special that I should remember?"

Vita reached behind the bar and grabbed her by the throat. "What makes me special is that I'm the only one who will break your fucking neck if you don't tell Wolf that Vita out here waiting on him!"

"Why didn't you say that in the first place," the old woman croaked. After giving her one last shake, Vita released her grip. "Wait here, I'll get him." The old woman came from behind the bar and disappeared into the back.

"That your idea of handling this with kid gloves?" Goldie asked sarcastically.

"I got no time nor patience for games."

"Whatever, I'm going to find a bathroom. I been holding my piss since we left Diamonds' place. Try not to kill anyone while I'm gone." Goldie went off in search of the restroom.

Vita sat at the bar, busying herself with her phone while waiting for Detective Wolf. Buda had been blowing her phone up, no doubt wondering where she and Goldie were. They were scheduled to link up at one of their stash spots on 136th and Eighth

Avenue. The building was across the street from the venue where they would be executing the hit on Big Stone. Vita had killed more than a few men and hadn't lost much sleep over them, but something about this just didn't feel right. There were still questions she needed answers to and she couldn't get them from a dead man.

Her thoughts then drifted to Domo. Buda had insisted that she made sure he was on deck, but why? She had a sneaking suspicion that Buda had somehow found out about his connection to the Stone family and was doing this as his ultimate test of loyalty. The thing was, Vita wasn't so sure this was a test that Domo would pass. If she didn't inform Domo of the mission, Buda would become suspicious and there was no telling what he would do to Domo, or her, for that matter. She thought about just telling Domo everything, but was afraid he would hate her for it, so honesty was out of the question, at least for the moment. She needed to find a way to ease Domo's hand out of the fire Buda had started without tipping either of them off. Just then she had an idea.

Vita had just finished texting Domo the location where she wanted him to meet her that night when she felt a presence behind her. She turned, expecting it to be Goldie returning from the bathroom or Wolf, but it was neither.

"So, we meet again." Knowledge smirked at her.

"Sorry, you must have mistaken me for someone else," Vita told him and turned back to the bar.

"I don't think so." Knowledge took the stool next to her. "You were at the hospital visiting Pops Brown."

"What are you, a cop?" Vita faked ignorance. She knew exactly who Knowledge was, but hadn't realized he knew her.

"No, just a curious young man," Knowledge told her. "When I first saw you I thought maybe you were one of Pops's kids, then I remembered he doesn't have any daughters. So I got to figuring maybe you were one of his young chippies, but then I saw the way he looked at you. It was almost as if he was afraid of you. Now what could an old-school gangster like Pops have to fear from some pretty young thing?"

"Look, why don't you get your nosy ass out of here before my boyfriend comes back from the bathroom and gets the wrong idea about our little chat, *yeah*?" Vita said, trying to hide the nervousness in her voice. Knowledge was toying with her, but to what end she wasn't sure.

"That's an awfully sweet accent you got," he said, ignoring her threat. "I got a thing for southern belles. What part of the south you from? Texas? Mississippi? No, wait, let me guess . . . New Orleans, right?"

Vita's hand dipped for the gun in her purse, but Knowledge was already on her. He yanked the purse away and twisted her arm behind her back, pinning Vita to the bar. "Take it easy, shorty. I just wanna talk to you."

"Fuck you." Vita threw her head back, smashing it into Knowledge's lip and forcing him to release his grip.

"I don't normally hit women, but if that's how you wanna play it I'm game." Knowledge rushed her.

Vita danced on the balls of her feet in a fighting stance. She waited until Knowledge had almost reached her, before sidestepping and catching him with two quick punches to the side of his head. From the expression on his face he had just realized that she was not only fast, but had a hell of a right cross. She tried the same tick again, but this time he was prepared. He blocked the blows and delivered one of his own to her gut, knocking the wind out of her. Before Vita could right herself, he tossed her over his hip and into a nearby table. Whatever fight she had left in her had officially fled.

"On your feet, my mysterious friend." Knowledge yanked her up by the arm. "I've been looking for you for quite some time. You and me are going to go outside and have ourselves a little chat." He shoved her toward the door.

"You don't know what you're getting yourself into, Knowledge," Vita capped.

Knowledge stopped short. "How the hell do you know my name?"

"Me knowing your name is the least of your concerns at the moment," Vita taunted him.

Knowledge was about to press her for more information, but he never got the chance. Something cracked over the top of his head and the world went loopy. When Knowledge came to, he was sitting on the floor propped against the bar with Power patting his cheeks. There was no sign of Vita.

"Knowledge, you good? Talk to me!" Power insisted.

"Yeah, I'm straight." Knowledge pulled himself to his feet. "What the fuck happened?"

"I don't know, man. I saw a chick and a dude running out of here so I came in to check on you. I found you laid out on the floor with a broken pool stick next to you."

"We gotta find that bitch. I know she's connected to everything that's been going on," Knowledge said heatedly.

"Man, later for that. I'm sure that old bartender already called the police after y'all busted her joint up. I think it best if we leave before they arrive."

"Too late, because they're already here," someone called from behind them. In the doorway stood a lanky, brown-skinned man. He had an angular face and keen eyes that seemed to look everywhere at once. His thick sideburns and deeply cleft upper lip gave him a canine appearance. With his hair in cornrows and his baggy jeans cuffed over his Timberlands, he looked like your everyday corner boy, but the badge hanging from around his neck said that he wasn't. "Which one of you dipshits were looking to howl at the moon?"

CHAPTER NINETEEN

Domo was tired by the time he made it back to Newark. Normally he would walk the mile or so from Newark Penn Station back to his block, but after the day he'd had he didn't have it in him so he hopped into one of the idling taxis.

Riding down Market Street he busied himself watching people hustling in and out of the busy rows of stores. It had been several years since they had revamped the strip, but the transformation still amazed and puzzled Domo. The city had gone out of its way to rebuild that part of the city to draw income from the tourists and, in turn, the shop owners, but had left most of the residential areas untouched. Houses in dire need of repair littered several blocks, while vacant lots where the city had torn down all the housing projects dominated others. They kept promising to rebuild on the properties and relocate the families they had pushed out during the demolition, but it had been a few years and they still hadn't gotten around to it. Newark was the only city where you could go from sugar to shit in less than a block, but it was home for Domo.

He had the taxi drop him off a block or so from his house,

and walked. Domo had been doing that a lot lately whenever he was in a taxi or riding in a car with someone. He never had them drop him off directly in front of his house. It was a habit he had picked up since he started running with Buda's gang: never let anyone get too close to where you laid your head. The front of the corner liquor store was busy as usual. It was a popular spot where the locals congregated to shoot the breeze or ply their respective trades. In the center of the gathering, decked out in a tan dickey suit and black Chuck Taylors, was Domo's friend and new business partner, L.A.

L.A. was somewhat of a staple in their neighborhood. He was only a few years older than Domo, but had been involved in the streets since he was in middle school and had already achieved OG status. He was a wild and unpredictable dude who was down to do anything in the name of a dollar. From robbery to murder, L.A. was with it. It had been L.A. who first plugged Domo into the New Orleans crew when he invited him to ride shotgun on a job. It was supposed to be a one-time thing, but now Domo found himself in so deep that he wasn't sure he could get out if he wanted to.

"What's up with you, young blood?" L.A. greeted Domo through a haze of Black & Mild smoke.

"Ain't shit. I'm just getting back from New York."

"I should've known that when I came by your house this morning and you wasn't home that you was probably laid up with Vita. You been up that chick's ass since I introduced you."

"I was actually handling something with Buda and them," Domo half lied. He didn't want L.A. any deeper in his business than he needed to be.

"Y'all went on a mission and didn't call me?" L.A. was

disappointed. He knew riding out with Buda meant quick cash, so he tagged along whenever possible.

"We tried to call you last night to run down the play, but your phone kept going to voice mail."

"Damn, my shit was dead until this morning. I had a wild-ass night with two broads from out of Candy Girls. Them bitches worked me out," L.A. said, reliving the night of wild sex in his head. "What y'all was on, money or murder?"

Domo gave him a look that said he knew better than to ask him that sort of question on a crowded corner.

"Damn, boy, you turning into a full-fledged savage out here on these streets. Looks like I created a monster." L.A. slapped Domo on the back good-naturedly. Sometimes it was hard to tell which one L.A. enjoyed more, putting in work or watching others get their hands dirty.

"What's popping out here?" Domo changed the subject.

"Shit, the block is jumping! That package Buda hit us with got these fiends out here going crazy. We almost out, and probably gonna have to go into New York to get hit off again soon."

"No need. We got a package coming in either tonight or in the morning. Some new shit," Domo informed him.

"So, what, you off making deals on your own now?" L.A. gave him a suspicious look.

"Nah, it ain't like that. Buda wants to push the stuff they came up on today out here. He's giving us half off too."

"It must be gonna snow in hell if that tight bastard is giving away discount drugs."

"I think he just don't want the shit Hank and Goldie stole traced back to them."

"Fuck it, I ain't gonna be one to block no blessing. Bring it on and let's get to this paper!" L.A. said.

"Speaking of paper, I'm gonna need my cut off of this week's profits. Got some things I need to take care of."

"Nigga, didn't you say you just did a job with Buda? Your pockets should be stuffed with cash," L.A. said.

"I didn't stick around for my cut. I'll pick it up tomorrow, but what I need to do ain't gonna wait."

"A'ight, I'll have someone bring it by your pad later on," L.A. promised.

"Nah, don't do that. Just call me and I'll come grab it."

"You moving awful careful these days." L.A. eyeballed him.

"You would be too if you'd seen what I have in the last week or so." Domo reflected on Oscar's face right before he killed him.

"I thought I heard you out here." Rah came out of the store carrying a forty-ounce Olde English 800 and a Dutch Masters cigar. His hoodie bore stains from whatever he was eating earlier that day, and his Timberlands were scuffed and flapping loosely on his feet. Raheem was a slob, but he was also Domo's best friend.

"Sup with you, Rah?" Domo gave him dap.

"Everything is groovy, beloved," Rah replied. "Yo, did this nigga L.A. tell you about Candy Girls last night?"

"You were there too?" Domo asked curiously. L.A. and Rah were cool, but he had never known them to hang out unless he was around.

"Yeah, L.A. treated a couple of the homies last night. Yo, my nigga was in there making it rain! You should've seen it."

"I'll bet," Domo said. He had been hearing here and there that

L.A. had been around town being flashy. They had both agreed to start keeping lower profiles in light of their new status, but it seemed only one of them was keeping up his end of the bargain. "Yo, I'll catch y'all in a few. I'm about to go to the crib and change my clothes right quick."

"A'ight, I'll have that for you by the time you come back out," L.A. assured him.

"I'll walk with you. I need to holla at you anyway." Raheem joined Domo.

The two of them walked down the street to the two-family unit in which Domo shared an apartment with his mother. They bounded up the stairs to the second floor, where their unit was located. When Domo opened the door the first thing he smelled was pine. This meant his mother had cleaned the house before she went out to work. It was a wonder she'd even had time, as much as she had been running around lately.

"So, what's good?" Raheem asked once they were inside Domo's bedroom.

"Ain't shit, man. Just taking it light," Domo said, sitting on his bed to untie his sneakers. It was then that he noticed the flecks of blood splatter on them.

"I see y'all got shit jumping out here," Raheem said, cutting to the chase.

"Really, and what makes you think that?" Domo asked, slyly kicking his sneakers under the bed. He would throw them out once he got a chance.

Raheem gave him a look. "C'mon, man. Everybody know you and L.A. holding that New York bag now."

"Is that what L.A. is saying?" Domo went to his closet and

began thumbing through his shirts. He had purposely not mentioned his involvement with the drugs to Raheem because the boy had a tendency to be chatty.

"He ain't gotta say it, he's *showing* it! Man, L.A. gave all them boys up on the corner packages to move for him. He offered me one, but I turned it down."

"How come?" Domo asked, pulling a long-sleeve black graphic T-shirt from its hanger. As long as he had known Raheem, he'd never turned down the chance to make a dollar.

"Because I ain't trying to be out there hustling dime bags, I'm trying to get it like you getting it," Raheem told him. He'd heard that Domo and L.A. were making serious money working with the crew from New Orleans and he wanted in.

"I'm making a few dollars here and there, but I hardly call that *getting it.*"

Raheem sucked his teeth. "C'mon, my nigga, this is me. I've been your ace since day one so you know you can't hide nothing from me. Put your boy down."

"Rah, you know it ain't that simple," Domo told him while scanning the dozen or so boxes of sneakers stacked against his wall, trying to figure out which ones to wear. "Buda and them are playing on a different level, and I don't know if it's such a good idea for you to get involved."

"Bruh, why you acting like I can't handle myself?"

"You mean like you handled yourself when I took you to meet them for the first time?" Domo reminded him.

Diamonds' cousin T.J. had thrown a baby shower for his girlfriend at T.J.'s house and Vita had *requested* his presence. Raheem had been on Domo's back for an introduction since Domo had hooked up with the crew so Domo figured that night would be as good as any. Of course Raheem had made a mess of it. He had foolishly gotten involved in a dice game with Buda and the two had exchanged words over a debt, and Buda had demanded he and Raheem shoot the *fair one*. Raheem was scared shitless by the brute and was making both himself and Domo look bad in front of Diamonds, so Domo stepped up for him. It was one of the worse mistakes he'd ever made. Buda had beaten him so bad that the bruises on his ribs had only recently started to heal. Domo had taken an ass whipping, but he'd also fought back and it earned him the respect of the crew. The same couldn't be said for Raheem. Because he hadn't stood up for himself the crew had branded him weak, which was the real reason Domo didn't want to bring him back around. He wanted to spare Rah the embarrassment that surely awaited him in the circle of bandits.

"That was just a big misunderstanding. Me and Buda are good now, right?" Raheem asked hopefully.

"Sure, Rah," Domo said and went back to scanning his sneaker boxes. He was about to remove a pair of Jordan's when he noticed something was off. Domo stood back and studied the boxes for a minute before it finally hit him. Domo always kept his sneaker boxes stacked according to brand, but now they were arranged according to box size. His mother had been in his room. Frantically, Domo began snatching the boxes away from the wall, looking for a specific one.

"Fuck is wrong with you?" Raheem asked, looking at his friend toss sneakers left and right.

Domo ignored him and kept searching. His heart thudded in his chest, fearing the worst. Finally he found what he was looking for, a tattered New Balance box. He breathed a sigh of relief when he flipped the lid open and found his secret stash of cash intact. For a minute he'd feared his mother had found it.

"Damn, that's gotta be about ten grand!" Raheem spooked Domo when he appeared hovering over his shoulder.

"Not even close." Domo flipped the box closed and tucked it under his arm.

"What did you do, knock over a bank or something?" Raheem pressed him.

"Nah, man. Just been putting a little money away here and there. Been saving up for something," Domo told him. "Yo, do you think your stepdad will let you borrow his car?"

"No, but at this time of day he's probably passed out drunk. It ain't shit to slip in the house and take the keys. Why? What's up?"

"I need a ride somewhere."

After collecting his money from L.A., Domo went back to Raheem's house to appropriate his stepfather's car keys. The old-timer was so drunk that he hardly noticed Raheem's sneaky hands fishing around in his pocket. From there Raheem and Domo hit Route 22 West.

"So, where are we going?" Raheem asked.

"Out to Union, like I told you," Domo said in frustration as he dropped the money back into the shoe box and started counting it over again. Raheem's mouth had been going since they left and he wished his friend would shut up. Domo's cell phone vibrated in his pocket, messing up his count again. He pulled it out and looked at the caller ID before sticking it back in his pocket without answering.

"That's the second time since we been together that your phone ring and you didn't answer. Who you ducking?"

"Nobody," Domo lied. Stoney had been calling him all day. No doubt by then Pearl had told her brother she had seen him, and Stoney probably wanted to know why Domo had been right in his backyard and hadn't so much as called him or stopped by. Domo felt bad about it and planned to reach out to Stoney, but only when the time was right. Domo wasn't yet sure which way the winds of his life were going to blow and he didn't want to get Stoney caught up in the bullshit he had going on.

After about a half hour of driving they had arrived at their destination, a small used-car lot out near Springfield Township.

"I'll be back in a second." Domo got out of the car with his shoe box in tow and walked into the small office.

Raheem also got out of the car and leaned against it, smoking a Black and waiting for his friend. After about fifteen minutes or so Domo came out of the office wearing an ear-to-ear grin. The shoe box was gone, replaced by a set of car keys and a temporary license plate.

"Oh shit, why didn't you tell me you were buying a car?" Raheem asked.

"Wasn't sure if I was going to go through with it. Ran into some extra money, so I said fuck it. I'm getting tired of riding public transportation at all times of the night back and forth to New York."

"That's what I'm talking about. We about to be riding in style!" Raheem said, as excited as if he had just been the one to purchase a vehicle. "Which one did you cop? Wait, don't tell me . . . that red joint right there." He pointed at the candy-apple-colored Honda Accord that was sitting on the lot. "Yeah, I know your style."

"Nah, not that one. Come on, I'll show you." Domo lead Raheem through the rows of cars to the very end of the lot. When Raheem saw the car his friend stopped in front of, he thought he was playing a joke. It was a piss-yellow Mustang that was at least fifteen years past its prime. It had a dented hood, with rust coating almost an entire side.

"You have got to be kidding me. I know you didn't just drop that box of money on this piece of shit?" Raheem couldn't believe it.

"Yeah." Domo smiled. "It's a piece of shit, but it's mine." The Mustang would not only be Domo's very first car, but it was the first major thing in his life that he had ever owned. It could use a little TLC, but by summertime he would have it looking like new money. He was proud of his first purchase and couldn't wait to show it to Vita. Domo's phone vibrated in his pocket again. With a sigh, he pulled it out, expecting Stoney again, but to his surprise it was a text from Vita. As usual it was short and to the point with only an address and a time. It was time to get back to work.

CHAPTER TWENTY

Diamonds was awakened by the feeling of soft kisses being planted on his chest. He cracked one tired eye open and found himself looking down at a mop of beautiful black hair. The kisses went lower and lower, over his stomach and finally tickling the line of hair just above his penis.

"Girl, best not start something you can't finish," Diamonds warned her.

She turned her face to him. She looked almost angelic with her alabaster skin, and full red lips. "Do I ever?" she asked before placing him in her mouth.

His whole body went hard as she began sucking, slowly at first and then faster. Every so often she would pop him out of her mouth, only long enough to explore the thin skin between his nuts and his asshole with her tongue. If Diamonds could bottle and sell the things she did with her mouth he'd be a rich man. Waves of pleasure rocked his body as he felt himself about to explode, but he would have no such release, at least not yet.

"Not so fast." She stopped, and gripped the head of his dick, keeping him from ejaculating. "You don't get to get yours until I get mine," she said and mounted Diamonds.

At that moment there was a heated debate going on in his head over which felt better, her pussy or her mouth. She rocked back and forth on his dick, finding her rhythm. He reached for her, but she pushed his hands away and pinned him to the bed by his wrists. As she rode him, Diamonds found himself lost in her twinkling green eyes. He could stare into them forever and never get tired. She began to ride him faster, her juices beginning to run down over his balls and onto the sheets. She was reaching her climax, as was he.

"Tell me that you love me!" she demanded.

"I love you," he rasped.

"I don't believe you." She slapped him across the face. "Say it like you mean it!" She bucked harder.

"I love you! Sweet Jesus, I love you, Bleu!" Diamonds howled as he exploded inside her. She came at nearly the same time. After she had released herself, Bleu collapsed onto his chest, listening to his heart beating. "You know I really do love you, right?"

Bleu rolled off of him and lay on her side. "Silly boy, don't say things you don't mean. That's just the sex talking."

"I do." Diamonds propped himself up on his elbow. "You think I go around killing men for women who I'm just trying to bed? This thing I feel for you is real, baby. Every time I'm away from you it's like a sickness, eating me up on the inside. You know Auntie thinks you worked some kind of hex on me."

"That old woman always up in my shit." Bleu snorted. "Only reason she always muddying my name is probably because she got designs on you herself. And maybe you got designs on her?"

"Nah, I like 'em old, but not as old as Auntie. She like a second mother to me. She raised me and Goldie up from nothing, and gave me power." He stroked the pouch around his neck.

Bleu laughed as if it were the most amusing thing she had ever heard. "Them parlor tricks that woman teaching you out there in the swamp ain't no real power." She ran her hand along his jawline and he felt a spark of electricity. "I could teach you a few things, but I don't think you ready. Maybe when you finally grow to become a man."

Diamonds pushed her hand away and sat up on the bed. "I'm more of a man than that nigga I freed you from. What he done for you besides kick your ass and keep you caged like some bird?"

"He give me all this finery." Bleu motioned around to the large master bedroom. "Mo wasn't the best man I had, but he wasn't the worst either."

"You say it like you miss that nigga! You want I should go out to where I buried him and raise him up again?" Diamonds asked angrily.

"Hush with that foolishness." Bleu pulled him back down on top of her. "You know these eyes don't see nothing but you. So long as you loyal to me, I'll always be yours, Diamonds."

"And I, yours, Bleu," he said sincerely. Diamonds hadn't known Bleu long, but in that short time he had come to love her more than he had ever loved anyone or anything in his life.

"Then prove it to me." She grabbed a fistful of his dreads and tugged hard enough to send pain through his scalp. "Make love to me with your mouth like I taught you."

"It would be an honor." Diamonds beamed before crawling down between her legs. He had just begun exploring her insides with his tongue when a pair of strong hands grabbed him by his ankles and yanked him off the bed. Diamonds hit his chin on the bedpost before being bounced off the floor. In a daze he looked up and saw several men standing over him, holding guns. "What the fuck is this?" he asked; he had never seen them before.

The lead man, who was tall and sported a beard almost as thick as Buda's, addressed him. "This is about a conniving whore and the games she likes to play. Get that bitch!" he ordered his accomplices. The men moved forward and dragged Bleu kicking and screaming from the bed.

"No! Get your hands off me!" Bleu fought against them.

"Shut up, bitch!" one of them roared before socking Bleu in the gut and taking the fight out of her.

"I'll kill you!" Diamonds sprang to his feet and charged the man who had just hit Bleu. A rifle butt to the head knocked him back to the floor before he could reach his target.

The bearded man grabbed a handful of Bleu's hair and yanked her head back. "You must've worked the same trick on this fool lil nigga that you worked on my uncle to have his nose open enough to die over you," the bearded man said. "You tell your little boyfriend that you make it a habit of bewitching young and dumb niggas into doing your dirty work?"

"That's a lie! I love her and she loves me!" Diamonds declared.

"Lil nigga, she got your head good and screwed up, yeah?" The bearded man gave Diamonds a sad look. "Don't worry, shorty. In time it'll pass. As for this bitch," he banged Bleu's head against the wall, "when I'm done she won't be working any more of her juju on anybody else. I can promise you that." He began dragging her out of the bedroom.

"No, you can't take her!" Diamonds tried to get up, but two of the men had jumped on him and were holding him down.

"Diamonds, help me!" Bleu pleaded, but there was nothing he could do. The men holding him down were far stronger than he was.

"Don't leave me, Bleu!" he cried. "Bleu! Bleu!" he screamed over and over, watching helplessly as the bearded man dragged his true love from his life.

PRESENT DAY, LIBERTY ISLAND

"Diamonds? Diamonds, can you hear me?" A pair of hands were shaking him.

Slowly the fog began to roll back from Diamonds' brain as he came back to consciousness. He looked around and found that he wasn't in the bedroom, trying to fight to save Bleu, but back in the cell Big Slim had tossed him in. Minister was staring down at him with a worried expression on his face.

"That must've been some nightmare you were having," Minister said, retaking his seat in the chair near the bed.

"I guess," Diamonds said, trying to sit up but realized he couldn't. His wrists were now cuffed to the bedrail.

"After that last stunt you pulled, Slim figured it would be best not to take any unnecessary risks."

"Smart man," Diamonds agreed.

"Who is Bleu?" Minister asked, to which Diamonds gave him a questioning look. "You were screaming her name in your sleep."

"Nobody for you to be concerned about," Diamonds said flatly.

"I get it, you don't want to talk about it. We can talk about something else. I heard about your little failed escape attempt. Did you really think you could get out of here with a bedspring being your only weapon?" Minister asked with an amused look.

"I'd have much rather had a pistol, but whatever works." Diamonds laughed.

"I'm glad you think it's funny, because Blue sure didn't. He's going to need a couple of stitches in his neck," Minister told him.

"If I had it to do over again I'd have slit his fucking throat."

"I'd be careful with that one if I were you. Blue ain't nothing to play with," Minister warned. "The only reason you're still alive and not floating around in that water out there with your skull cracked is because Big Slim still wants you alive."

"Fuck Slim and his games. Why don't he just kill me already?"

"That, I can't say for sure. It's above my pay grade. Best advice I can give you is to play nice until this is all over."

"Minister, you've been in here picking my brain long enough to know that ain't even in my nature. Big Slim letting me live is going to come back to bite him in the ass before long. I'm either gonna bust out of here on my own, or my crew is gonna find me. Buda probably got them out there on the trail as we speak, and when they finally track me down it's over for that fat muthafucka," Diamonds said confidently.

"I wouldn't hold my breath on that last outcome. I get the impression that right now the only one concerned about you staying alive is Big Slim," Minister told him, reflecting on his meeting with Buda. It saddened him that Diamonds had so much faith in a man who didn't give a shit about him.

"And what's that supposed to mean?" Diamonds asked. Before

he could receive an answer, a searing pain shot through his gut, causing his body to seize. It only lasted for a few seconds but it felt like it went on for hours. When it finally passed he felt spent.

"When I got back I checked the stitches you busted. That infection looks like it's getting worse. I fear if you don't get proper medical help soon you won't have to worry about Big Slim killing you anymore."

"You don't know the half," Diamonds wheezed. "So, where'd you get off to earlier?" he asked, changing the subject to take his mind off the poison that was ravaging his system.

"Had to run into New York to handle some business."

"I noticed something while talking to you, Minister. You got an accent that kinda comes and goes as it pleases. Where about you from, the Carolinas, maybe Georgia?"

"Close, but no. I'm actually from Florida. Born and raised in Jacksonville. I moved to Miami a few years ago to start a personal security company with my brother."

"I take it that didn't go so well, seeing how you're up here doing dirty work for a piece of shit like Slim."

"Actually, we were pretty successful with it. Everybody from rappers to athletes paid us top dollar to keep them safe when while they were in Florida. I closed the business down and started freelancing about a year ago."

"If you were doing so well with the company, why shut it down?" Diamonds asked.

"I don't know, I guess after my brother was killed my heart just wasn't in it anymore."

"I'm sorry to hear that, truly."

"Thank you, Diamonds. I don't know why I didn't see it coming, though. See, my brother was a man who liked to dance between two worlds," Minister began. "We were making legitimate money hand over fist, but he just couldn't seem to let go of his street ties. I was in Atlanta for about a month doing some extended work for a rich client we had just taken on when I got the news. While I was away my brother had hooked in with some gangsters in Miami. He was always out and about partying with them in places he knew he had no business being in. I'd warned him against it, but my brother was hardheaded that way. Seems he had become really close with some of them. One night they were at this club called Onyx and some guys got into a shootout. My brother wasn't involved, just in the wrong place at the wrong time."

Diamonds searched his memory bank. "I remember that shootout, happened a few summers back."

"Everybody heard about it. The damn thing made all the newspapers."

"Nah, I didn't hear about it. I was there," Diamonds corrected him. "I lost a good friend that night too, but he wasn't no security guard. My buddy was a stone-cold gangster. I met him not long after me and mine touched down there and started doing our thing. He was kind of a liaison for us while we were down there. Knew all the ins and outs. He was no slouch when it came to putting in work either. Boy saved my ass more than a few times. He was the closest thing I had to a friend that wasn't born in New Orleans. The night he was killed we were at Onyx celebrating his initiation into our crew. I eventually tracked down the nigga who shot him and took my time bleeding that boy before I dumped his ass in the swamp and left him for the hungry things that lived out there."

"Bet that made you feel better, being able to avenge his death,"

Minister said, wishing he had been able to lay hands on the ones who had killed his brother. By the time he had arrived back in Florida the culprit had vanished.

"For a time, I guess it did. But between me, you, and these walls I'd rather have my partner back. Friends like Rasul ain't easy to come by these days." Diamonds reflected on his old running buddy. The next thing he knew Minister was out of the chair and hovering over him.

"What did you just say?" Minster asked in a tone that made Diamonds uneasy. He was now almost nose to nose with Diamonds.

"Listen, friend, I don't know how comfortable I am with a muthafucka this far in my space unless it's a pretty girl. Why don't you back up just a taste so I can make sense of what you getting at?" Diamonds said coolly.

Minister grabbed Diamonds by the hair and slammed his head against the cot twice, before drawing his gun and shoving it under his chin. "On everything I love, if you don't shoot straight with me, I'm gonna say fuck what Slim wants and blow your damn brains out!" He rained spittle over Diamonds' face. "Where'd you get that name?"

"Minister!" Blue called from the doorway. Minister had been so focused on Diamonds that he hadn't even heard the door open. "Why don't you take it easy. Big Slim wants to see him."

"Fuck you and fuck Slim. Me and this one ain't done talking!" Minister said over his shoulder.

"Oh, but I think you are." Tariq eased up behind Minister and put his gun to the back of his skull.

"Minister," Blue began in an even tone, "I really like you, kid.

So please don't make me let Tariq end you. Take a walk and cool off."

Minister weighed his options. He could probably take Diamonds out and still stand a pretty good chance of finishing Tariq, but Blue would cut him down before he made it across the room. Dying wouldn't get him the answers he still needed. "We'll finish this conversation another time." He gave Diamonds a gentle slap before holstering his gun and backing off. "He's all yours," he said to Blue as he passed him on the way out.

Blue had Tariq cover Diamonds while he unlocked his cuffs and pulled him to his feet. "I've never seen Minister lose his cool like that. What did you say to piss him off?"

"I'm still trying to figure it out myself," Diamonds said before allowing himself to be escorted from the cell.

Diamonds felt like every bit the prisoner he was, being shuffled through the hallway with his hands and feet shackled. Minister wasn't joking when he said they weren't taking any more chances. Now that he wasn't fleeing for his life he could take better stock of his surroundings. He was somewhere on Liberty Island, this much he could tell from spotting the statue during his escape attempt. Instead of a road to freedom, Diamonds had found himself standing in the shadow of Lady Liberty. Vita had made him take her to see the statue when they had first gotten to New York. It was one of the most popular tourist attractions in the state and was always bustling with people, and security, so how Big Slim had managed to hold him there without their being noticed was yet another of the great mysteries in his life. As he thought on it, he did recall from his trip with Vita seeing some buildings that were closed due to the fact that they were under construction, so it stood to reason that he was somewhere in that area. Now that he had figured out where he was, his next move would be to get word to his people so they could bust him out.

Blue and Tariq led him up a winding stairwell to an open room. The windows were covered in plastic as the glass hadn't been installed yet so there was a bit of a draft. Through the plastic covers he could see the Manhattan skyline. *So close, yet so far,* he thought to himself. In the center of the room, speaking to several men whom Diamonds had never seen before, stood his one-time boss and now archnemesis, Big Slim. What felt like a lifetime ago, Diamonds and his crew had worked as muscle for Slim's heroin cartel in New Orleans. During Hurricane Katrina, Diamonds had given Slim his two weeks' notice by way of putting several bullets in him and stealing his drugs before fleeing New Orleans. It had seemed a foolproof plan, but the one thing Diamonds hadn't accounted for was Slim surviving the assassination attempt.

"If it isn't the Prince of Thieves." Big Slim smiled when he saw Blue and Tariq walk in with a shackled Diamonds between them. He made a dismissive gesture and the minions he had been talking to left the room. "You know, for a time I never thought I'd live to see this day, Big Chief Diamonds bound and at my mercy."

"Don't get too caught up in the moment, Slim. It ain't gonna last," Diamonds said defiantly.

"And why is that? You expecting that gang of backwater bumpkins you run with to storm this place and rescue you like in some action movie?" Big Slim laughed. "I doubt that. They've got their hands full at the moment, but we can talk about that later. Take a seat." He motioned to an empty chair in the center of the room.

When Diamonds didn't move, Slim motioned to Tariq, who swept Diamonds' legs out from under him and sent him crashing to the floor.

Diamonds tried to get up but was overcome with vertigo so he only made it as far as a kneeling position. His condition was getting steadily worse.

"You don't look so good, bruh," Big Slim taunted him.

"Got a touch of the flu, is all," Diamonds lied. "I'll be plenty fine when it comes time for me to cut your heart out, fat man."

"Same old Diamonds, defiant to the end." Big Slim chuckled. "You can play tough all you want, but I think we both know that you're on borrowed time, thanks to this." He pulled the black dagger from his jacket pocket. Diamonds' eyes lit up at the sight of it. "What, you didn't think I knew what this was and what it was capable of?" He twirled the knife in his hands. "I tried to buy this thing from Auntie a few times, offered her good money for it too, but she would never sell it. Good thing I was able to take it off you for free. To be honest, I'm impressed you've lasted this long. The poison in this blade would've killed most men within the first three days, but you're proving to be full of surprises, aren't you?"

"Why don't you just kill me, fat man, so I ain't gotta listen to your annoying-ass voice anymore."

"Oh, you're just as good as dead, but it'll be when I say and not a moment before. I got plans for you, dear boy. See, when I tracked your slimy ass to New York I had intentions on just taking you out for what you did to my people and for them bullets you put in me, but when I saw the little lane you had opened up for yourself I saw an opportunity to make back what you took from me and then some. What I started in New Orleans, I will finish in New York."

"You think these New York niggas are going to let you waltz in out of the blue and set up shop?"

"Of course not, which is why it's fortunate for me you've already laid all the groundwork. You already ripped out all the weeds, so I figure why not let you plant the fresh crops too?" Big Slim capped.

Diamonds laughed. "Slim, you must've fell and bumped that big-ass head of yours. I told you before I aired you out the first time that I was done working for you."

"You did, and sounded damn sincere when you said it. Yet the universe has saw fit to bring you right back to the foot of my table, waiting for me to drop some crumbs. By this time tomorrow your boys will have received the first shipment of heroin from your new suppliers and start distribution in the territories promised to you by Eddie, right before you turned around and bit him like the snake you are."

Diamonds shrugged. "So, you keep up on current events. I'm still waiting for you to get to the part where I give a fuck. Whether I'm there to see it through or not, that ball is in play and ain't shit you can do to stop it."

"Why would I stop it when I can capitalize off it? In all your peacocking around making plans to be the next king of New York, you never once stopped to ask yourself how such a sweet deal fell into the lap of a dumb country nigga like you?" Big Slim asked.

"You trying to tell me it was you who set me up with the connect?"

"Even better, it's my dope they'll be hitting you with," Big Slim said smugly.

"Bullshit!"

"No, real shit," someone called from behind Diamonds.

When Diamonds turned to see who had joined the party, he had to do a double take. The man's baggy clown clothes and cowardly demeanor were gone, replaced by a tailored black suit and a cold sneer. "Rolling?" Diamonds asked in disbelief.

"Good to see you again, Diamonds. I just wish it'd been under different circumstances," Rolling said, adjusting his tie.

"You sold me out? I knew you was a two-faced snake the minute I laid eyes on you!" Diamonds spat.

"Then you should've followed your instincts," Rolling told him honestly. "See, me and Slim go back a little ways. When my brother exiled me from New York I found myself in limbo, floating from state to state, hustling where I could, and eventually found myself in New Orleans. This is where I met Slim and he helped me start making some real money. When I got my weight up I made my way back to New York to settle the score with my brother, then I started hearing about this bad-ass cowboy who had some of the most dangerous men in the city hiding under rocks. It was pure coincidence that you happened to be the same person who tried to kill my benefactor. Slim wanted to kill you immediately, but I convinced him to let you live. At least until you killed Big Stone for me. I saw the value in having a rabid dog at our disposal, and then you fell for my niece and became a liability, and had to be removed from the chessboard."

"You think my crew gonna let this fly? Buda and my team gonna hunt you like dogs when they find out about all this."

"Buda?" Rolling laughed. "Who do you think signed off on all this?" He removed a recorder from his pocket and pressed *play*.

"We'll call this the icing on the cake. The minute I lay your brother out, you have to lay mine. Diamonds has to die."

Hearing the recording from the meeting made Diamonds feel physically ill. He didn't want to believe what Slim and Rolling were feeding him, but the voice on the recording was undeniably Buda's. The man he had loved like his own brother had sold him out just to get his position.

Big Slim looked down at Diamonds. "You feel that, Diamonds? The lump forming in your throat threatening to choke you? That's hopelessness. Killing you wasn't good enough. I needed to break you first. Now I'll let you die." He waved Blue and Tariq forward. "He's all yours, boys. Wait until I'm gone then flush this piece of shit."

"With pleasure." Blue beamed. For what Diamonds had done to him, his death would not be quick or pretty.

PART

IV

RED RAIN

CHAPTER TWENTY-ONE

Domo had just enough time to get an oil change and a fresh wash for his new bucket before heading back to the block to get ready to meet Vita and the others. He had to admit that the sudden way in which this new plan had arisen had him concerned. The crew was usually cautious before they moved on someone, scouting them first, and this seemed to come out of the blue. It wouldn't have been the first time he'd taken on a spontaneous caper with them since he joined up, but something about the way this one was going down felt different.

Raheem wanted to go joyriding in the Mustang, and when Domo told him he had something to do it opened the door for Rah to start asking a million questions. He knew there was something Domo wasn't telling him. Rah's pestering went on until Domo dropped him off on the block. Domo promised to clue him in, but Raheem was already in his feelings about being left out, which seemed to be the norm with him lately. When Raheem got out of the car he didn't even give Domo dap before leaving. Domo would deal with his emotional friend later. He needed to get ready.

When Domo got back to the apartment he was surprised to find his mother home. She was in the kitchen frying up some chicken and talking on the phone. Domo waved hello and tried to slide into his room, but Carla motioned for him to stay put. He could tell from her body language that something was bothering her. Domo let out a sigh. He was pressed for time and the last thing he needed was one of his mother's lectures making him later than he already would be. He leaned against the kitchen door and waited for her to finish with her call.

"Where you just coming from?" Carla asked once she was off the phone.

"Nowhere special. Just running around with Raheem," Domo told her.

"I should've known." Carla snorted. "I don't want that boy in my house when I'm not here."

This surprised Domo. "Ma, Rah comes over here all the time and you've never had a problem with it. Did he do something?"

"It's not about what he's done, it's what he might do that worries me. That boy has been moving around real funny lately. I went to the store the other day and when I came back I found him nosing around on our stoop."

"Maybe he was about to check and see if I was home," Domo reasoned.

"That's possible, but from the guilty-ass look on his face when I caught him, I doubt it. To add to it I've been seeing him spending a lot of time around that greasy-ass guy L.A. lately, and we all know how he gets down. I heard a story about him robbing his own mama, and a man like that ain't got no hang-ups about who he steps on. Don't be hanging around them too much because I don't want you catching any part of what they surely got coming to them. I can smell it on those two."

"Ma, you acting real strange. Is everything okay?"

"That's what I'm trying to figure out, Domonique." That Carla had called him by his full first name meant it was about to get serious. "Look, I'm too tired to dance around the issue so I'm just gonna come out and ask you: Are you out there doing things you don't have any business doing?"

"Of course not." He faked ignorance.

"Don't bullshit me, Domonique!" Carla's voice was heavy with emotion. "I'm giving you the opportunity to come clean now rather than have me get blindsided by the police later."

"Ma, I have no idea what you're talking about. I mean, you know I keep a little side hustle going here and there, but I'm not into nothing crazy."

Carla folded her arms. "So you're standing here trying to tell me that sixty-five hundred dollars came from you doing side hustles?"

She had found his shoe-box stash.

"Ma, before you get all crazy let me explain—"

"I don't even wanna hear it, because I know anything that comes out of your mouth next is going to be a damn lie. You know, if we've never had anything else in this house we've always had trust. I can go out there and work for thirteen and fourteen hours a day and not have to worry about you so much because I trust you to make good decisions, but apparently that trust has been misguided."

"But you're not even trying to let me explain," Domo insisted.

"Finding a shoe box full of money in my unemployed teenage

son's room pretty much explains itself. I just hope you ain't been stupid enough to stash no drugs in this apartment. You know we can't afford to lose this place."

"I would never do anything like that. You should know better." Domo was hurt at the accusation.

"At this point I don't know what you're capable of, Domonique, I know we ain't got much but I bust my ass from sunup to sundown so that you won't have to be in the streets throwing stones at the penitentiary. I know I can't always get you the latest sneakers or clothes, but I provide you with a roof over your head and food in your stomach."

"Why should you have to provide me with anything?" Domo asked, a bit sharper than he intended. "Ma," he softened his tone, "do you have any idea how hard it is for me to sit back and watch you work your fingers to the bone and not be able to do anything to help out? It was killing me, so I went out and did what I had to do."

"You know, you sounded just like you brother when you said that." Carla shook her head sadly. "That's the same shit he used to pop before the police caught up with him and tossed him in prison. But maybe that's what you want, to end up like your brother, or worse, your father?"

"My brother got caught up because he was with a crew of dumb niggas, and don't even get me started on my sperm donor. I ain't never gonna be a nigga who abandons his kids." Domo's father was a sensitive issue in their house and they rarely talked about him.

"Sometimes the streets don't give you a choice," Carla shot back.

"You sound like you're defending him." Domo gave his mother a look.

"Boy, you know better than that. Your father was a bastard for leaving us without a pot to piss in, while he set his other three kids up in that mansion, but God settled his tab. I'm just sorry his eldest got caught in the crossfire because kids are innocent. Domonique," she took his hands in hers, "the point I'm trying to make is the streets have already taken enough from me, and you getting in the game will open the door for them to take the last good thing I got left."

"That's not going to happen to me," Domo promised. His cell phone vibrated in his pocket. He looked at the screen and saw a text from Buda: *How long?* It was almost game time and he wanted to make sure Domo was still in. *40min,* Domo replied and put the phone back in his pocket.

"Who was that? Raheem, maybe L.A?" Carla asked.

"Nah, this girl I've been seeing. I got a date tonight," Domo lied.

"Domonique, maybe you should stay in tonight. I got a bad feeling in my spirit."

"Ma, you bugging. We ain't gonna do nothing but go to the movies and get something to eat."

"Then why don't you invite her here instead?" Carla's voice was almost pleading. "I'll cook for you guys and we can rent some movies now that the cable is back on."

"Okay, I'll hit her up and see if she's with that." Domo started toward his bedroom.

"Domonique," she called after him. "I hope that you know that I ride you so much because I love you."

"I love you too, Ma," Domo said and shut his bedroom door.

Carla collapsed on her living room couch and let out a deep sigh. She felt like the weight of the world was on her shoulders, and it was. She was pissed at Domo, but she couldn't say that she didn't understand, probably better than he gave her credit for. She too had to sit by and watch her mother struggle to raise her and her siblings on her own, and this is what had pushed her into the streets so young. It was also that need for a man's love she had been deprived of as a child that pushed her into the arms of both her useless babies' fathers. One thing Domo had been wrong about was him being nothing like his father. He was more like Thomas than he would ever truly understand and that's what scared Carla most. The call of the streets was strong in his ears and she knew he was at an age where he could go in either direction. Domo might have Poppa Clark's genes, but she would fight until her dying day to make sure that her son never lived his father's life.

Carla had just finished frying the chicken and was thinking about baking a cake for Domo and his company. She went to his room to ask him what kind she should make. She knocked on the door and when she didn't get an answer, she figured maybe he had gone to sleep so she went inside. Carla's heart broke when she found Domo's bed empty and his window open.

CHAPTER TWENTY-TWO

"About damn time you two got here," Buda said to Vita and Goldie when they walked into the apartment. He was hunched over the coffee table loading a machine gun.

"We ran into a problem. Me and Goldie went to the meet with the Wolf, and ran into an unexpected guest," Vita told him.

"What the fuck did you go see that pig for?" Buda asked suspiciously.

"We were following up on a lead about Diamonds."

"What'd he say?" Buda questioned, hoping the detective hadn't somehow foiled his plans. If anyone could get to the truth of what had become of Diamonds it would be that bloodhound.

"I never got a chance to speak to him because Knowledge showed up," Vita said in frustration.

"You think the detective tipped him off? Maybe cut a side deal with these niggas?" One-eye Willie asked. He was perched by the window, with a rifle mounted on a tripod facing the street. He looked anxious.

"At this point, I don't trust no-fucking-body." Vita was talking to Willie, but had her eyes on Buda.

"As you shouldn't," Buda told her, chambering a round into the gun he had been loading. "I don't know why you even wasted your time when I already gave Goldie the word about what happened to Diamonds."

"But that's the thing: I have reason to believe that Diamonds isn't dead at all. I went by Diamonds' place today and his car was in the garage, still in his spot. Not only that, I also found his cell phone and there were some text messages in there that I'm still trying to make sense of. Buda, I think we need to put this on hold until we get all our ducks in a row."

"Maybe she's on to something," Lucky added. He was sitting in a chair across from Buda, smoking a blunt. His face was calm, but his eyes were dancing in his head. He was nervous.

"Man, later for all that weak shit the both of you are talking." Buda waved his hand dismissively. "At this point, whether he's dead or alive ain't gonna stop what needs to happen. Everything is in place and we come too far to not go through with it. Everybody strap up, we need to get into position."

"Say, where's Hank?" Goldie asked, noticing for the first time that he was absent from the war party.

"I ain't seen him since he left the spot this morning," Willie said.

"He check in with any of you?" Goldie asked the others but no one had heard from him. "How the fuck the OG go missing all day long and nobody don't think to check up on him?" he pressed heatedly.

"Relax, Goldie. Me and Hank got into it this morning so he's probably still in his feelings. We don't need him to pull it off. Domo can play his role tonight. You did call on him, right, Vita?" Buda shifted the focus. He watched her face closely to see how she would respond.

"I spoke to him a while ago. He's running behind so he'll meet us at the spot, but he'll be there," Vita lied. "Why you so hell-bent on making sure he rides on this one?"

"He's a part of this crew, ain't he? Everybody gotta earn their keep. Besides, for the stakes we'll be playing for soon I need to know how the young boy is built. This here will be his baptism of fire." Buda stood. "Now if everybody is done giving me the third degree, let's load up and go lay these niggas out."

Buda watched over his team like a proud father while they armed themselves and prepared for the coming battle. All of their months of careful planning were finally about to bear fruit. Rolling had been right when he said that Diamonds had laid out a perfect plan, but it took Buda to execute it. He couldn't wait to see his friend's face when he broke the news to him that he had done what he couldn't. He would give Diamonds a minute to savor the taste of crow before he took his life.

"Buda, I need to rap with you for a minute." Vita broke him from his thoughts. Goldie and Lucky had already left the apartment, but she lingered behind.

"Sup, V?" he asked in a tone that said he clearly didn't want to be bothered.

"I think we're about to make a mistake. This shit was poorly planned and too many things can go wrong. We're about to step out of the shadows and declare war on the kings of New York; if even one of them escapes to tell the tale we're going to have every crew in the city on our backs," Vita pointed out.

"Then I guess you better make sure your bullets ring true, lil sis." Buda sneered. "You know, I don't recall y'all second-guessing Diamonds this much. You, Hank, and the rest followed him into the bowels of hell on more than one occasion without so much as a question and I'm starting to feel I ain't getting that same respect."

"That's because Diamonds always had a sound plan."

"Well, Diamonds ain't chief no more, now is he?" Buda shot back. "Look, V, this shit is going down with or without you. Now I'm going downstairs with the real niggas to set this off. If you're by my side, I'll know you're with us. If not," he patted his pistol, "I'll know you're not." He walked off.

After Buda had gone Vita continued to stand there, weighing what she was about to get herself into. Every fiber in her body told her that they were making a bad move, but what choice did she have? Buda hadn't said it directly, but his message had been received: she could either join her crew in battle or be branded a traitor and a coward. Neither option sounded appealing. Her cell phone went off, and her face fell when she saw Domo's number on the caller ID screen. She hoped that one day he would understand that whatever the outcome, she'd had his best interests at heart. Hitting *ignore,* she went off to join the fight.

Domo had a lot to process on his ride into New York. He felt bad about slipping out on his mother, but she just didn't get it. He had watched her suffer long enough and had vowed that he wouldn't sit idle anymore. He had chosen his path and hoped that she understood.

He made it through the Lincoln Tunnel in record time. He was already running behind and didn't want to hear Buda's mouth about him showing up late for a job. He had no idea who they were about to take off, but by that point it didn't too much matter. He navigated the streets until he found the address Vita had texted him. Had had to double-check it to make sure he had read it right, but he had. It was an abandoned warehouse in the meatpacking district. What the fuck could they be taking off in there?

Domo waited for twenty minutes or so, but still hadn't seen any sign of the crew and was starting to get worried. He tried calling Vita but the phone just rang. When he tried to call her again it went straight to voice mail, as if she had powered it off. Domo began to replay the entire day's events and something wasn't adding up. What if instead of this job being his final test, Buda had something more sinister planned for him? It could've been paranoia on his part, but something wasn't right with the setup and he had no plans of sticking around to figure out what it was.

CHAPTER TWENTY-THREE

As promised, Big Stone made sure Pearl's party was of epic proportions. It was held at his restaurant, Rain, which was located uptown on Eighth Avenue. It was a nice spot that had a dining area on the lower level and a club on the second floor. Out front spotlights flashed HAPPY BIRTHDAY PEARL in the sky.

"Wow, don't you think this was a bit much for a teen party?" Asia asked as she and Knowledge pulled up to the front of the venue.

"Ain't nothing wrong with a man spoiling his kids. We're gonna do the same for ours when we have them."

"And have them turn out like Pearl, thinking everything in life is given and not earned?" Asia sucked her teeth. "I don't think so."

"Why don't you just be cool. I know you and Pearl don't always see eye to eye when you're at work, but this isn't St. Francis High School, this is her birthday party, and I expect the both of you to be civil."

"So long as she doesn't get out of pocket," Asia said. "How's your head, baby?" She touched the knot on the back of his skull, causing him to flinch.

"It'd be fine if you'd quit picking at it."

"I will when you tell me how you really got it," Asia shot back.

"I told you, I fell," Knowledge lied. When it came to his street business he kept Asia on a need-to-know basis. She wasn't naive about what he did, but the less he told her the less likely she was to be charged with conspiracy if he ever got bagged.

"That's bullshit and you know it, but I'm gonna let you have that. At least for tonight." Asia clicked her tongue on the roof of her mouth.

The valet met the Range Rover and opened the doors for the couple. Knowledge got out first. He was wearing a black suit, white shirt, and paisley tie. His lady was looking equally good in a flowing blue strapless dress.

Sandra was standing out front talking to Big Stone and Black when she spotted Knowledge and Asia. "Well, well, well, don't you look handsome." She kissed Knowledge once on each cheek. "Boy, if I was a little younger you might be in trouble."

"Quit playing before you get me in trouble." Knowledge laughed. "Sandra, I'd like you to meet my girlfriend, Asia."

Sandra gave Asia the once-over then nodded in approval. "You're even more beautiful than Knowledge told me. I can see why he's been hiding you, probably because he's worried about somebody stealing you."

"Thank you." Asia blushed. "Is the birthday girl here yet? I'd like to give her the present from us." She held up a gift bag.

"Yeah, she's inside cutting up with her friends. Come on." Sandra looped her arm in Asia's. "Let's go inside so I can show you where to put the gift and we can grab some drinks. I'm sure the boys got business to discuss anyhow," she said, leading her toward the entrance.

"Damn, that's a fine piece of woman." Black whistled as Asia walked inside.

"Don't get your old ass kicked out here, Black," Knowledge said playfully. "Sorry I'm late, boss," he addressed Big Stone. "Kinda had my hands full."

"I still can't believe you let a girl kick your ass." Black laughed.

"She didn't do shit, and had her buddy not hit me from behind I'd have beaten the information we needed out of her by now," Knowledge said angrily. He was still in his feelings about Vita escaping.

"Well, hopefully you'll get your rematch soon. Any luck with Wolf?" Big Stone asked.

"It would've been easier getting blood out of an orange. He admitted to getting a dude named Buda out of jail on behalf of one of his *clients,* but wouldn't tell me who. Claims it's confidential information," Knowledge told him.

"Sounds like a crock of shit to me," Black added. "Well, if this Buda character got tossed out of a whorehouse, it means he's in the business of paying for pussy and y'all know that's my field of expertise. I'll have my girls keep their ears to the streets. We'll find this janky muthafucka."

"So, is everybody here?" Knowledge asked.

"Yeah, they're back in the kitchen area," Black told him. "Everybody who was confirmed to show up did, except one."

"Eddie," Knowledge guessed.

"Boy, you must be psychic," Big Stone joked.

"Not at all. This thing has had his stink on it from the beginning," Knowledge said. When he'd met with Eddie the week before to inquire what he knew about the bandits, he'd faked ignorance, but the fact that he'd been MIA ever since said that he'd known more than what he was telling. "I should've blasted his ass right then and there."

"Eddie's time will come, son. Once we consolidate our forces we'll deal with this Buda nigga and everybody else who didn't wanna get with the program," Big Stone vowed. "Like Black said, I got everybody tucked in the kitchen so as not to make Pearl suspicious. You know that girl is nosy as hell. We need to hurry up and get back there before my daddy bores them to death with his old war stories. I ain't never met a nigga who loves to hear the sound of his own voice like Bo Stone." Big Stone shook his head.

"I could think of one," Knowledge teased.

Big Stone gave a half chuckle. "Very funny, nigga. Now bring your ass on so we can get this meeting started."

The birthday party was happening upstairs, but in the kitchen a gangster party was taking place. Knowledge walked in to find at least a half dozen cats that he knew by name or reputation congregating around a stainless-steel counter. To the average person this gathering of elder statesmen didn't seem like much, but they represented what was left of those who hadn't fallen under or in line with the new threat plaguing the city. Big Stone had put out the call to arms, and they had answered.

There were some heavy weights in that room, all powerful and well respected in their trades, but the one who had the most presence had been the only one who could say he'd played the game and lived to retire, Bo Stone. Bo looked like a miniature version of Big Stone, being shorter than his son by almost a foot and nearly half his weight. He was still in good physical condition, but nowhere near the monster he had been in his glory days. Knowledge had once heard a story about Bo Stone hitting a man so hard that he shattered every bone in his face. He was a beast back then, but old age and bypass surgery had slowed him down.

"Well, it's about damn time you brought your ass back in here, Stone. I thought we were gonna have to listen to your daddy's tired-ass stories all night long," Isaac said. He was an old-timer who moved heavy coke in Staten Island.

"Isaac, you just mad because in your best days of slinging poison your money couldn't stand up to what I made of my protection rackets," Bo Stone capped. When he was in the streets he made ten cents off every dollar made in the neighborhood.

Isaac sucked his teeth. "Man, you wasn't but a well-spoken goon, taking that community-uplift shit. How you uplifting the community when you're charging for your services?"

"The cost to be the boss." Bo chuckled.

"Well, if you old heads are done strolling down Memory Lane, can we get to it? Some of us got other shit to do tonight," Born said. On that night of all nights, Rain was the last place he wanted to be, but Big Stone had insisted. Born was one of his street bosses and was supposed to serve as sergeant at arms in times of war. Born had started to make up an excuse and thought of just plain blowing it off, but Rolling had convinced him otherwise. He was to be Rolling's eyes and ears on the inside to help coordinate the assassination. Born didn't like it, but he had accepted the task and hoped that Buda's people were as good a shot as they claimed to be.

"Boy, what the hell is wrong with you tonight? You been acting all jittery since you got here," Big Stone pointed out.

"Sorry, boss. It's just that I got a little jump-off lined up and the bitch keeps blowing my phone up trying to figure out what time I'm coming to get her." The lie rolled off Born's tongue.

"That bitch can wait. We got pressing business we're here to discuss," Big Stone told him.

"Then how about we get on with it?" Richie suggested. He was a fence and a thief who ran a crew of jack boys from the east side. Nothing went missing around the city that Richie didn't steal personally or know who stole it. He was a sneaky dude and the least liked of those in the room.

"Right on," Big Stone concurred. "Fellas, it's no secret why I called you here tonight. We've got a serious problem brewing in the streets."

"*Serious* is an understatement. I hear they're trying to put you *poison pushers* on the endangered species list," Bo Stone capped.

"Daddy, I really ain't up for your shit tonight. As a matter of fact, I don't even know why you're at this meeting instead of upstairs at the party. This is for active hustlers," Big Stone said slyly. He and his father had never had the best relationship and the older they got, the more it seemed to deteriorate. "While my daddy is over there cracking jokes, like mass murder of our friends and loved ones is funny, I'm trying to put together a solution. I say we pool our resources and meet this threat with numbers."

"Join forces under whose banner, yours?" Richie scoffed. "Stone, you ain't never offered to share a cab let alone your resources, and now you wanna play United Nations because these boys got you on the ropes. I think this is just another plot for you to get us all under your thumb like you've been doing for years. Frankly, me and mine are prepared to hunker down and wait this shit out."

"If that were true then you wouldn't be here," Knowledge spoke up. "Look, fellas, it's no secret that there's been some bad blood between several of us in this room over the years. We're all drug dealers and this city ain't but so big, so it's to be expected we step on each other's toes from time to time. It comes with the territory. But for all our differences we now have a common enemy, and that's these niggas out here cutting the heads off of all our friends and associates. I say that shit stops tonight."

"I hear you talking, youngster, but how are we supposed to combat an enemy we can't even identify?" Isaac asked.

"That was true, up until now," Big Stone informed him. "Knowledge has been out hitting these streets harder than Mike Tyson in his prime and he was able to uncover a few things about our mysterious enemies."

"One of them goes by the name of Buda," Knowledge picked up. "Thick muthafucka with a beard who goes in for the whores. He keeps company with a slim brown-skinned dame, known to be pretty good with a trumpet, and a tall joker who rocks a bandanna around his neck." He recounted the descriptions Power had given him after he was ambushed in Midian.

"Sounds like the ones who raided my spot and killed my boy," Snow Man interjected. He was an older man who had gotten his nickname not from his long white beard but from the grade-A cocaine he pushed. "About a year ago they got the drop and took us off for ten bricks. Those bastards tied me up and made me watch while one of them gutted my son like cattle with a black knife. Until the day I die I'll remember that diamond-toothed smile mocking me from behind that ski mask while he killed my boy," he said emotionally.

"Did you say diamond-toothed?" Knowledge asked curiously.

"That mean something to you?" Big Stone asked.

"Was just a hunch until now." Knowledge went on to tell them of the man called Diamonds whom he had encountered sniffing around what remained of Pops's bar. He purposely omitted the part about the man having been with Pearl.

"And you're just now thinking to mention this?" Big Stone asked angrily.

"Let me play devil's advocate here," Isaac interjected. "I'm sure I speak for every man in this room when I say we've been trying to get a read on these boys for months, yet you seem extremely knowledgeable about them. Maybe it's you and Big Stone who turned these dogs loose on the city in the first place? Who's to say this isn't some elaborate scheme you two cooked up to get us to play ball?"

"It's a valid concern, Isaac, but ain't no truth to it," Big Stone told him. "Just this morning they took out two of my biggest cash cows. Everyone in this room knows how much I love money so could you see me cutting my nose off to spite my face like that? I gotta be honest with you boys, any doubt I had about these dudes being a real threat died when I heard they cut Pana's heart out in broad daylight. I can't speak for the rest of you but I ain't never encountered no muthafuckas as vicious as these, and frankly, I'm worried, as we all should be. Now whether we partner up or not, every man in this room is going to have their day in court with this crew. I'd sooner do it in numbers rather than keep getting picked off one by one."

"Now that's one thing we can agree on," Richie said. "Me and my boys are in."

Knowledge stood off to the side and watched as one by one the heads of the crews signed off on Big Stone's plan to consolidate their forces to go at the outsiders. It had been a brilliant plan on Big Stone's part. He had seen what Diamonds and his lot could do and knew they would need all the help they could get if they planned on beating them. As Knowledge continued his silent observation, something stuck out to him. All of the heads of the crews were present, but besides him and Born their captains were absent. Maybe Big Stone had made it a closed-door meeting and neglected to tell him and they were upstairs at the party, but it was something Knowledge would look into as soon as the meeting let out.

"That went better than expected," Big Stone told him, once the meeting was over.

"Of course it did. For all the shit these niggas talk, they know there's strength in numbers and that's what we need right now. If we're done here, I'm gonna go upstairs and check on Asia. Ain't no telling what kinda foolishness Sandra is putting in her head," he joked.

"Hold on a second, and come with me to walk these old niggas out, then we can go up to the party together. Besides, I need to bend your ear about something real quick." Big Stone draped his arm around Knowledge. "For what you pulled off in there, you just earned yourself a promotion."

CHAPTER TWENTY-FOUR

Sandra escorted Asia to the upper level of the club where the party was taking place. It had an ocean theme, and the club was decorated in blues, greens, and golds with fish swimming in the glass dance floor. It didn't take them long to find Pearl. She was in the middle of the dance floor with Marissa and two boys who looked like they were way too old to be at a teen's birthday party. Pearl was looking like every bit the princess that she was in a form-fitting gold dress with matching tiara. She was grinding on one of the boys, giving him the business, while the crowd cheered her on.

"My eighteenth birthday wasn't nothing like this," Asia said, taking in the humpfest.

"And hers won't be either." Sandra bumped her way through the crowd in Pearl's direction.

Pearl was so deep into her groove that she hadn't even noticed that the crowd had gone quiet. She turned around and was about to try a move she had seen in a music video on the guy she was dancing with, but he was gone and she found herself confronted with an angry Sandra. "Oh, shit." She covered her mouth.

"*Shit* is one of a few words that come to mind right now. What the hell are you out here doing, looking like you're at a burlesque show instead of a birthday party?" Sandra scolded her.

"I was only dancing."

"Looks like you were trying to get pregnant," Sandra capped. She sniffed Pearl and caught the unmistakable smell of alcohol coming off her. "Girl, have you been drinking?"

"I might've had one glass of wine. It is my birthday, after all," Pearl half lied. She had indeed had only one glass of wine in the club, but that's after she and Marissa had been doing shots of Hennessy in the back of the limo on the ride over.

"Bullshit, your ass is tipsy!" Sandra fanned the alcohol fumes.

"Damn, is that Officer Jones!" one of the boys in the crowd shouted. All the kid's heads seemed to whip around at once, putting Asia on the spot.

"What's she doing here?" Pearl asked with a major attitude.

"Pearl, what the hell is wrong with you? This is a guest. Show some respect," Sandra demanded.

"Oh, I know just who Officer Jones is. I just wanna know why she's at my party." Pearl folded her arms.

"It's Asia tonight. I'm off the clock. And I'm here because my man invited me." Asia matched her tone. The little girl was out of pocket as usual and Asia was trying her best to keep from slapping her and turning the whole party out.

"Your man?" Pearl was confused.

"Yes, Pearl. This is Knowledge's date, Asia," Sandra explained.

"Wait, this who he wifed up?" Pearl asked in disbelief. Of all the women she expected to come to her party that night, security officer Asia Jones was the last person who would've come to her mind. Knowledge was a street dude and powerful, while she was just average.

"Do you two know each other?" Sandra finally caught on.

"Yeah, she's a security guard at my school," Pearl said.

"Part-time, sweetie. I'm actually finishing up culinary school." Asia winked just to piss her off further.

"That's cute. Maybe my dad will hire you to work in his kitchen," Pearl said smugly.

Asia was about to say something nasty, but caught herself. "You know what. I'm going to head over to the bar and grab a drink." She turned and walked off. It was all she could do to keep from putting hands on Pearl.

"You were way out of line, Pearl!" Sandra said angrily. "You're going to apologize to that girl."

"No, I'm not. I don't care if she is sucking Knowledge's dick, she'll always be nothing but the help and needs to know her place. Fuck him and fuck her!" Pearl slurred, loud enough for anyone listening to hear. Though all she and Knowledge had had was a childhood crush that would likely never go anywhere, she still couldn't help but feel betrayed to see he had given his heart to someone else. The fact that it was someone she knew and saw every day in school made it sting worse. It was the second time in as many weeks that she'd had her feelings stomped on.

"Okay, now I know your ass is drunk. Time for you to get some air and sober the hell up." Sandra grabbed Pearl roughly by the arm and dragged her down the stairs.

Big Stone was standing just inside the entrance when he saw Sandra pulling Pearl along behind. He could tell by the look on

Sandra's face that she was heated. "Everything okay?" he asked as they drew closer.

"Yeah, just taking Pearl to get some air." Sandra downplayed it.

Big Stone caught a whiff of Pearl. "Is she drunk?"

"I ain't drunk, Daddy. Just a little tipsy." Pearl flashed him a goofy grin.

"Jesus on the cross, I can't go one night without some bullshit!" Big Stone threw his hands up in frustration.

"Don't worry, I got her," Knowledge said, reaching for Pearl. To his surprise, she recoiled.

"Keep your dirty hands off me. I don't want you touching me after you been touching that bitch," Pearl hissed.

"Huh?" Knowledge was caught totally off guard.

"All you niggas are the same," Pearl continued. "You make girls fall in love just so you can laugh when you shit on them. I would've given you all of me, do you know that?" She was yelling at Knowledge, but in her mind, she saw Diamonds.

"Come on, ladies." Bo Stone stepped between them, slipping one arm around Pearl's waist and the other around Sandra's.

"I hate you, nigga!" Pearl spat at Knowledge before allowing her grandfather and Sandra to escort her outside.

"Something you need to tell me about?" Big Stone asked Knowledge coldly.

"Man, you should know me better than to even ask that question. I have no clue what that shit is all about," Knowledge said honestly.

"We can talk about it later. Let's get these fools in their cars and wrap this up before my drunk-ass daughter makes me do something crazy." Big Stone pushed the doors open and stepped outside.

The valet had just begun to pull the first of the cars up when Knowledge finally came out. Big Stone was standing on the curb having a conversation with his new allies. A few feet away, Sandra and Bo were holding Pearl up while she vomited on the curb. Knowledge couldn't remember seeing her that drunk. When she sobered up they were definitely going to have a talk about her performance.

He scanned the sidewalk in search of Born. He needed him to hold Big Stone and the others down while he went upstairs to check on Asia. There was no telling what Pearl's drunk ass had said to her and he needed to make sure his lady was good. After five minutes of searching, he realized that Born was nowhere to be found. Knowledge and Big Stone had been standing at the foot of the stairs, so he'd have seen him if he had gone up to the club. He was gone, but why would he up and leave without saying anything? Knowledge's question was answered when Isaac's head exploded, spraying blood over Big Stone.

"It's a hit!" one of the men who had been working security at the door shouted.

Knowledge didn't even think about it before he drew his gun and rushed to Big Stone's side. He tackled the larger man. He and Big Stone hit the ground just as a bullet shattered the window of the car Big Stone had been standing next to. Knowledge swept his gun back and forth, looking to see where the shooting was coming from, but didn't see anyone. He went to peek over the car, and another bullet slammed into the hood. It was then he caught a glimpse of a figure in the apartment window across the street.

"Sniper!" he shouted, to let the rest of the security team know where the shots were coming from. "I gotta get you inside," he told Big Stone.

"Fuck me, I'm good." Big Stone produced a revolver from the ankle strap hidden under his pants leg. "Get my daddy and the girls to safety."

"But Stone—"

"Go!" Big Stone shoved him away, and fired over the top of the car at the window.

Knowledge got low using the cars for cover and made his way to the Stone family. Bo had pulled them behind a mailbox and was covering them with his body. Thankfully they were all still in one piece. "Come on, I'm gonna get you guys to safety," he shouted over the gunfire.

"Knowledge, what's going on?" Sandra asked.

"I don't know, but we'll figure it out once I get you inside. On my signal, everybody break for the restaurant door. Ready?"

"My daddy, somebody has got to get my daddy!" Pearl cried. She was now completely sober and terrified.

"Pearl, look at me." Knowledge took her face in one hand. "I'm gonna get to your father, but I can't do that until I make sure you guys are safe. Do you understand?"

Pearl nodded.

"Okay, just stay low and don't stop moving until you're back inside Rain," Knowledge told them. "Okay . . . now!" He leapt up from behind the mailbox and started blasting at the apartment window. Knowledge backpedaled, laying cover fire while Bo, Sandra, and Pearl scurried through the doors of Rain. On the ground in front of the club were at least four dead bodies, but thankfully none of them was Big Stone. A flicker of motion to his right drew Knowledge's attention. He saw four people, three guys and a girl, creeping in his direction. Their faces were covered, but he didn't need to see them to know who they were. His rematch had come sooner than he had expected.

"Damn that One-eye Willie!" Buda cursed when he heard the first shot from the rifle. The plan had been for Willie to wait for the ground forces to get close before he opened fire, but of course he had jumped the gun and ruined the element of surprise.

"Well, since they already know we're here, might as well get to it." Goldie laughed. "This is for my brother, niggas!" He charged forward, firing his machine gun.

"Goldie, wait!" Vita called, but he was already gone. Vita tried to go after him, but Buda stopped her.

"Stay focused, gal! Our target is Big Stone. Everybody else is a bonus," Buda told her before surging forward.

Vita was trailing Lucky, who was creeping up on Big Stone from his blind side. They had him trapped. For a second it looked like Lucky would be the one to claim the prize for the night, before Big Stone turned and put a bullet in his face. He was dead before he hit the ground. Vita looked up to see Knowledge holding the smoking gun. Her heart swelled with rage, as she added her gun to the fray trying to take Big Stone out.

The front of Rain ran red with blood, as bodies littered the street. All of the bosses who had attended the meeting were dead with the exception of Big Stone. He was crouched behind a car, gun raised and breathing heavy. It seemed like enemies were descending on him from everywhere at once. He looked to Knowledge, who was pinned behind a car by a barrage of machine-gun fire from the bandanna-clad man in the middle of the street. Big Stone was about to move to try and lay cover when a masked man stepped on the curb. The gunman had him dead to rights, but he hesitated, which gave Big Stone enough time to put a bullet through his face.

Behind him Big Stone could see two more masked hitters coming his way. He raised his gun, but it clicked empty. He looked from the trapped Knowledge to his would-be assassins and made a difficult choice.

"He's trying to run!" Goldie shouted when he saw Big Stone pop up from behind a car and bolt down an alley. He made to go after him, but Buda stopped him.

"He won't get away that easy. You just keep these niggas off our backs, we'll take care of Big Stone. Come on, V," Buda barked as he took off down the alley behind Big Stone. The moment he had waited so long for was finally at hand and he wouldn't be denied.

Big Stone's heart thudded in his chest as he ran down the alley between the club and the building next to it. He felt bad about leaving Knowledge, but he didn't have much of a choice. It was either that or stay there and die with him. If they were both killed there would be no one left to extract revenge, and after what had happened at Rain there would definitely be a reckoning. All he had to do was make it through the alley to the next street over and he would be home-free. All thoughts of freedom faded from his mind when he saw that someone had blocked the mouth of the alley with a Dumpster. He was trapped.

"Don't rush off just yet, the party is just getting started," Buda called to him as he stalked down the alley. Vita was on his heels, eyes sweeping back and forth for more enemies.

"Where's Diamonds?" Vita pressed him.

"Who the fuck is Diamonds and what does he have to do with me?" Big Stone asked.

"It was you who sent your people after him. Tell us where he is and we might let you live," Vita replied.

"I can't tell you what I don't know," Big Stone insisted.

"Shut your lying-ass mouth!" Buda barked before shooting Big Stone in the knee and dropping him. "You took our brother out and now we're gonna take you out!"

"You're free to kill me, but it ain't gonna change the fact that I have no idea who or what you're talking about," Big Stone pressed.

"Fuck it, he ain't gonna talk. Do this nigga, V!" Buda ordered.

"Maybe we should take him with us and question him first. If Diamonds is still alive we don't wanna ruin the best chance we got at finding him," Vita said.

Big Stone looked back and forth from Vita to Buda, and the realization of what was happening set in. "Baby girl, I hate to be the bearer of bad news, but it seems to me that somebody has played you. You got my word on two things here today: the first being that I don't know anybody named Diamonds and the second being I'm going to make it my business to find him when this is all over with. If you kill me now it's gonna open a faucet of blood that neither of is going to be able to turn off."

"I guess that's a chance we're just going to have to take," Buda told him before shooting Big Stone in the head.

"What the fuck, Buda? You killed him before we even had a chance to question him. He could've told us where Diamonds was!" Vita snapped.

"V, I never needed Big Stone to tell me where Diamonds was because I've known this whole time," Buda revealed. "He's dead, same as you are." He pumped two slugs into Vita's chest.

CHAPTER TWENTY-FIVE

Goldie was slapping a fresh magazine into his machine gun when he saw Buda come out of the alley. A smile crossed his face because he knew that Big Stone was dead and the score had finally been settled. He wished that he'd been the one to end the crime boss, but would have to take his victories where he could. After few seconds had passed and he noticed that Vita wasn't with him, the smile faded.

"Where's V?" Goldie asked frantically. The saddened look on Buda's face confirmed his suspicions. "No," his eyes welled with tears.

"I'm sorry, Goldie. Big Stone got the drop on us in the alley. She died saving my life," he lied. "But don't worry, I settled up for her and Diamonds. Now we best get outta here. Police gonna be on the scene any minute."

"We can't just leave her there for the rats. Vita was a warrior and deserves to be sent off as such." Goldie started towards the alley, but Buda stopped him.

"Boy, you gone plum mad?" he grabbed Goldie by the shirt.

"That girl is gone and ain't the living can do for the dead except honor their memories. And the way we do that is by becoming kings of this city like Diamonds and Vita wanted. Let's make their deaths count for something."

"Fuck them pigs and fuck this city. You've got your pound of flesh, but I ain't going nowhere until I get mine," he shoved Buda away and started stalking towards Rain.

"Goldie!" Buda called after him, but he was ignored. When Goldie's mind was set to do something, nothing short of God could change it. A trait he definitely shared with his older brother. Maybe if Buda was lucky, Goldie would get himself killed pursuing Knowledge and save him the trouble of doing it later.

Knowledge was crouched behind the car, trying his best to avoid the hellfire spewing from Goldie's machine gun. Every time he tried to get up to get off a clean shot, he nearly got it knocked off. In the distance, he could hear police sirens closing on their location, but he doubted they'd get to him in time.

There was a brief pause in the shooting. He peered through the ruined window of the car he was hiding behind and saw one of the two masked bandits who had chased Big Stone into the alley? Where was the other one? The masked bandit exchanged words with the machine gunner, and based on his reaction he wasn't delivering good news. The gunman was tugging at the machine-gunner, and for a second Knowledge was hopeful that they had been spooked by the approaching sirens and would leave. That hope died when she saw the machine gunner shake loose and start in his direction. He checked the magazine in his own pistol, three bullets left. He didn't stand a snowball's chance in hell, but at least he would die trying.

"Fuck it," Knowledge came up from behind the car, and fired two blasts. The shots were taken off balance, and neither hit their mark. Knowledge barely made it back behind the car before a spray of bullets perforated the hood. His heart thudded as he heard glass crunching on the other side of the car. The machine gunner was moving in to finish him off. He'd missed his mark. One other side of the car, Knowledge heard the sounds of glass being crunched as the machine gunner moved to finish him off. Knowledge readied his gun and prepared to meet his end the same way he had lived, like a gangster. Before his moment arrived, there was another gun added to the fray.

When the shooting started, the inside of Rain erupted into bedlam. Party-goers flew into a panic, with everyone scattering trying to get out of harm's way. The first thought that popped into Asia's head was Knowledge. She hadn't seen him since she came inside, but she knew if Big Stone was the target of whoever was shooting, her man would surely be the first one to try and place himself between the crime boss and danger. Without even thinking, she ran down the stairs in the direction of the shots.

She arrived on the main level to find it a mess of broken glass and blood. There seemed to be bodies everywhere, some already dead and some badly injured. She recognized some of them as kids who went to St. Francis. Her heart hurt for the phone calls their parents would likely receive before the night was over notifying that the children they had sent out to a birthday party would never be coming home again. A part of her felt guilty for being relieved that Knowledge wasn't amongst them.

"Get off me!" Asia heard someone scream. She looked over and saw a hysterical Pearl. Marissa and one of security team who hadn't been gunned down were trying to restrain her. On the floor next to them, Sandra was attending to an older man who was bleeding from the leg.

"What happened?" Asia approached them, looking around for answers.

"I don't know," Sandra answered. "We were all standing around outside when somebody started shooting. Oh, my goodness, those poor children," she fought back the sobs that came every time her eyes landed on the scattered bodies.

There was another spray of machine gun fire from outside causing everybody to causing everybody to duck. "Damn, it! They're killing our boys out there. Let me up!" Bo Stone tried to push to his feet. The killer in him fought its way to the surface, urging him to join the battle but his leg couldn't steady him.

"You ain't going nowhere on a busted wheel, Bo," Sandra pushed him back down, "and anybody poke their head out there is gonna get it blown off. Ain't nothing we can do for them at this point."

Pearl sat with her palms pressed over her ears, trying to drown out the sounds of the gunfire and screaming. She felt helpless, which had been the story of her life lately. Sheila's death, Devonte almost abducting her, and finally Diamonds abandoning her. All these things came at her in waves, and in each situation, there had been nothing she could do to stop them. She'd had enough of feeling like she was at the mercy of whatever fate life would dictate for her and it was time to take control. She pushed Marissa off her, and kneed the guy who had been holding her in the nuts, freeing her from his grip.

"Pearl, what the hell are you doing?" Bo called out, watching his granddaughter scramble on hands and knees over broken glass and bodies towards the door.

"For once in my life taking control of the situation," Pearl told him as she searched the bodies of the fallen security staff until she found what she was looking for; his weapon. Pearl pried the Glock .40 from his dead hand.

"Pearl, you're gonna get yourself killed!" Sandra yelled after her.

"Maybe," Pearl checked the clip, and slapped it back in just as her father had taught her, "but I won't be going alone," she stepped through what was left of the entrance.

Pearl didn't know what she had planned when she picked up that gun. Nor was she sure what she would do when she stepped out into something that was way out of her league, but the situation unfolding in front of her wouldn't allow time to sort either decision out. She arrived in time to see Knowledge narrowly escape a barrage of bullets that knocked smoked out of the hood of a parked car. The shooter was a tall man wearing a mask, inching towards Knowledge. Something about the set of his posture rang familiar to Pearl, but the sight of him raising the gun to finish Knowledge shifted her focus. Steadying her hands as best she could, she opened fire.

Knowledge watched in shock as the machine gunner's shoulder exploded in a spray of crimson. The gun discharged planting a

trial of holes in the concrete that stopped just short of Knowledge's feet. Another shot followed, and another after that sending
the machine gunner back peddling and tumbling onto his side
in the street. He struggled to his feet, fumbling with the machine
gun to let off another burst, but a car screeched to a halt and cut
off his line of fire. Reluctantly, the machine gunner allowed himself to be pulled into the car. Two more shots rang out, busting the
back window before the car peeled off into the night.

Knowledge was a man who believed more in science than he
did faith, but there was no denying that it was a miracle that had
saved him from a nasty death. He looked over his shoulder,
expecting to see one of Big Stone's soldiers, or Rain's security
team, but instead found Pearl. She was standing on the sidewalk,
holding smoking pistol still aimed in the direction the car had
fled in. There was a hard look in her eyes that Knowledge had
never seen before and it made him uneasy.

"Pearl?" Knowledge called out to her softly. She turned to
him and for a minute he thought she was going to start shooting
again. "It's okay," he approached her cautiously. "I got you," he
plucked the gun from her hand. "Are you okay?"

"No," Pearl's eyes went to her trembling hands. They were
smeared in blood and dirt from when she'd pried the gun loose
from the dead soldier. "My father?" she asked, realizing she didn't
see him anywhere.

"I got Big Stone. You just get back inside incase they double
back," he told her.

"No, these are our people," her eyes roamed over the corpses.
"I need to do something."

"These muthafuckas are gone," Knowledge motioned toward

the bodies. "If you wanna help, there's a lot of hurt folks inside that need tending to. Now go on," he nudged Pearl toward the door. Reluctantly, Pearl went back inside to help attend the injured. He waited until she was out of harm's way before going in search of Big Stone.

He cautiously approached the mouth of the alley, at the ready in case of any surprises. All seemed quiet as he ventured deeper. Knowledge had hoped Big Stone had made it to freedom at the other end, but that hope was dashed when he saw a pair of legs sticking out from behind a Dumpster. "No," Knowledge dropped to his knees over the bullet riddled body. The man who had been his father and mentor was now gone, leaving a void in his heart that could never be filled. At least Big Stone had taken one of his killers with him, Knowledge thought as he remembered seeing two people go in the alley after Big Stone and only one come out. His eyes swept the alley for a dead body, but all he found was a trail of blood leading to the other Dumpster, which was blocking the alley.

"Don't you fucking move!" a rough voice called from behind Knowledge. He cast a glance over his shoulder and saw several uniformed officers making their way down the alley. For an instant, he'd thought about holding court in the streets, but decided against it. In death, he could serve no purpose, and he still had unfinished business to deal with in life.

As the police lead Knowledge from the alley in cuffs, he took stock of the bodies spread out along the sidewalk. Nearly all of the remaining bosses of the city were gone, including his mentor. The irony was that they had been taken out by the very men they had been about to rally against. Most would've considered it dumb luck that their enemies had been able to catch them all slipping in once place at one time, but Knowledge knew better. The fact that nearly all their lieutenants had conveniently missed the meeting stank of an inside job. It had been a set up from the beginning and he cursed himself for not seeing it sooner. His eyes were open now and all he could see was red, and come morning so would the streets. It was open season on their enemies, starting with the traitor Born. Knowledge would kill him the ugliest.

The front of Rain was teaming with police and emergency vehicles. Spectators were lined up behind the yellow tape, likely curious to find out who or what had turned their neighborhood into a war zone. Photographers snapped pictures of Knowledge in chains and he already knew how it would play out in the morning paper. The man who had spent his life staying low key was about to be thrust into the spotlight.

While he was being shoved into the back of a patrol car, he caught a glimpse Pearl. She in front of the club being questioned by police, while Asia and Sandra stood watch. A sliver of a smile crossed his face, as he knew the police were wasting their time trying to pump Pearl for information. She knew better than to utter a word until she had a lawyer present, as Big Stone had trained her. What worried him was what would happen next. Pearl was a civilian, but she was still a Stone and now had to carry the burden of the name. So long as an heir to what Big Stone had built remained alive, they represented a threat which meant life was about to change for Pearl and Stoney. He only prayed they would be ready for what was to come.

As police car holding Knowledge was pulling away from the

curb, he made brief eye contact with Asia. Her face was solid, and defiant, but Knowledge knew that inside she was going to pieces and just trying to put up a good front for Sandra and Pearl. They had always discussed the possibility of him one day getting busted for how he lived, and the measures she needed to take in the event of an arrest, but the conversations had always been hypothetical. Seeing him in cuffs made it real. Before she faded from view, Asia gave her man a curt nod letting him know that she would do what needed to be done. Practice was over, and it was game time.

CHAPTER TWENTY-SIX

It had been a long night for the women of the Stone household. After being asked what felt like a million questions by the police, they were taken to the precinct to be asked a million more. For everything the police asked her, Pearl's answer remained the same: "I was inside when the shooting started and didn't see anything." In truth, she couldn't get the picture of the massacre out of her mind. The family lawyer, Abe Kauffman, finally showed up to the precinct at about 5 A.M. which put an end to the inquisition. After promising to return the following day for another round of questioning the ladies were allowed to leave with Kauffman.

Kauffman dropped Pearl, Sandra, and Asia at the brownstone in Harlem. Asia had wanted to go back to her apartment but Sandra convinced her to stay with them for the night. She was trying to hide it, but she was in bad shape after what had happened with Knowledge. They had been informed by Kauffman that they were trying to charge him with murder being that they had found him in the center of the crime scene still holding a smoking gun . . . the gun Pearl had fired. She wasn't sure if she had hit anyone or not, but now that Knowledge's fate hung in the balance she hoped that she hadn't. Still, even if they couldn't hang any of the bodies on Knowledge, the weapon's possession charge was enough to take him out of the picture until further notice. Every man any of them cared about had been taken away that night and all the women had left was each other.

Stoney was still asleep when they arrived at the brownstone. Pearl wanted to wake him up and break the news to her little brother that they were now officially orphans, but Sandra advised against it. She figured it would be best to put it off until the morning and Pearl reluctantly agreed. Sandra offered to be the one to break the news to him when he woke up, but Pearl said she'd do it. Sandra had been through enough so it was accepted the responsibility. She only hoped she had the strength to do it. For a time, Pearl just stood in his doorway watching her little brother sleep. He seemed so peaceful, likely dreaming about girls and video games. Little did he know that his whole world had just been destroyed.

On weary legs, she staggered to her bedroom. She was still covered in dirt and blood, but didn't have it in her to shower that night so she peeled off her ruined party dress and climbed into bed. Sleep didn't come easy to her. Every time she closed her eyes she saw the image of her father's corpse being wheeled out of the alley. She loved that man more than anything and he had been taken from her for reasons that she was still clueless to, but before it was said and done she would get to the bottom of it and deal with everything and everybody accordingly.

It felt like Pearl had just drifted to sleep when she was awakened by the sound of the doorbell. Head still in a fog, she started making her way to the stairs. In the hallway she was met by Stoney, who had also been awakened by the bell.

"Pearl, what's going on and why is there blood on your dress?" Stoney asked sleepily.

"Nothing, just go back to bed," Pearl told him before descending the stairs.

Sandra was standing in the doorway talking to someone. Asia hung back in the foyer, with her arms folded and a disgusted look on her face. Pearl peered over Sandra's shoulder to see who she was talking to. There were two uniformed officers and a woman dressed in a business suit. At first Pearl thought they had come to deliver more news about her father's murder until she heard Sandra yelling.

"What kind of bullshit is this?" Sandra snapped.

"Ma'am, would you please calm down," the woman in the suit urged her.

"Calm down, my ass! This family has suffered a terrible tragedy and y'all won't even allow us a moment to grieve before you come through here with this bullshit?"

"Mrs. Stone," the woman mistook Sandra for Big Stone's wife, "I'm sorry for your loss, and I assure you I don't want to be here anymore than you want me here. I'm just doing my job."

"What's going on?" Pearl asked.

"They come for Stoney," Sandra said fighting back the tears.

"What?" Pearl asked in shock. She was wide awake now. "What the hell do you want with my little brother?"

"Listen, I'll tell you like I told you mom, we had a report that a minor named Lenox Stone Jr. was residing at a residence deemed unsafe and we've come to remove him until we can investigate further. And from the looks of things I'd say those accusations weren't unwarranted," the woman looked at Pearl's bloody dress.

"Miss, this is all one big misunderstanding." Pearl tried to assure her.

"Misunderstanding my ass," a voice they were all too familiar with called from outside. Zonnie marched into view, dressed in a tight-fitting dress and heels that had no place on a woman's feet at that hour of the morning. "Y'all got my boy living in harm's way and I aim to do something about it!" she declared.

"Bitch, you can't be serious?" Sandra looked her up and down. "I been taking care of Stoney since he was a baby and now you wanna come back now that he's almost grown and play the concerned mother?"

"Wait, so you're Lenox Stone Jr.'s legal guardian? Meaning you can prove it?" the woman in the suit asked hopefully. She didn't care for the hood rat Zonnie and didn't want to remove the boy unless she absolutely had to.

"Well, yes I'm his guardian but not legally," Sandra told her. "I been taking care of these kids since they were small though. We were supposed to make it official on Monday, but—"

"But nothing," Zonnie cut her off. "You just said it yourself that you ain't got shit on paper. I'm Stoney's only surviving parent so my word chumps that of the family maid. Now y'all go in there and get my son!"

"Wait, how did you know that my father was dead?" Pearl asked suspiciously. It had only happened a few hours prior and

Pearl was sure it hadn't made the news yet. The guilty expression on Zonnie's face told the tale. She had been in on it. "You stinking bitch!" She lunged at Zonnie, but the officers restrained her. "As God as my witness you I'll kill you if I find out you had a hand in what happened to my father!"

"See, you heard her threaten to kill me with your own ears. I told you these people were unstable." Zonnie taunted.

"Zonnie, I know me and you ain't never seen eye to eye on much, but don't do this . . . at least not now," Sandra pleaded with tears in her eyes.

"Fuck you and your crocodile tears." Zonnie chuckled. "I'm taking my son out of this den of sin and come Monday you can expect to hear from my lawyers about what's owed to my son from his father's estate. I know that muthafucka kept a will or something."

Sandra's lip trembled with rage. For a second Pearl expected her to make one last attempt to plead with Zonnie, but when next she opened her mouth the only thing that came out of it was a glob of spit, which landed right on Zonnie's face. "You gonna rot for this, whore!"

"You saw that, she just assaulted me. I want her locked up," Zonnie said dramatically, while wiping away the spit.

"Ma'am, do we really need to make this situation worse?" the woman in the suit tried to plead with her.

"You can either arrest this bitch or I'll go to your supervisor and explain how you failed to do your job," Zonnie insisted.

With little other choice the woman in the suit gave the officers the nod to put Sandra in cuffs. When the other officer tried to come into the house to retrieve Stoney, Pearl stood to block his path, while Asia eased up behind him. The looks on both ladies' faces said that they were ready to take it wherever the officer wanted.

"Pearl," Sandra called to her. "It's okay. They've got a job to do and going about it like this ain't gonna help. We'll do it the right way."

Pearl didn't want to, but she reluctantly let the officer pass. The whole time he was searching the house for Stoney, she continued to glare and Zonnie. Zonnie was trying to look tough because the police were there, but when Pearl caught her in the streets she was going to jump in her ass. After about ten minutes of searching the officer came back empty handed, much to everyone's surprise.

"There's no one else here," the officer told them.

"Where are y'all hiding my son?" Zonnie demanded to know. No one spoke.

"Well, we can't remove a child if there isn't one on the premises. We'll try back another time." The woman in the suit gave Pearl a knowing glance. "And you can take those cuffs off Mrs. Stone."

"No the fuck you won't," Zonnie interjected. "I told you I want this old bitch locked up and I'm going all the way with it. She's going to jail."

"Gladly," Sandra said. "I'll only be in there for a few hours, but you'll be a bitter bitch for the rest of your days." She laughed and started marching towards the waiting police car.

"I'll get Kauffman back on the line and have you out right

away, Sandra," Pearl called after her. "Is there anything else you need me to do?"

Sandra stopped short. "As a matter of fact, yes. Prepare yourself accordingly, princess. These muthafuckas done declared war, and we're going to give them one!"

EPILOGUE

Domo breathed a sigh of relief with he finally made it back to Newark. He never in his life thought he'd be so happy to see The Bricks. It had been a long night and he longed for the comforts of familiar surroundings. His mother had been blowing up his phone since she discovered that he was missing from his bedroom. She was probably worried and pissed off. Domo shot her a text to let her know that he was okay, but he wasn't quite ready to talk yet. Even when he wouldn't find the words easily to articulate what he was going through. His mom was his best friend and one of the strongest people he knew, but how could a woman possibly understand what it was like to be a young man?

He passed through his neighborhood to grab some weed from one of the little dudes on the block. While he was out there he spotted Raheem and L.A. in the courtyard. A friendly face and a kid ear was just what he needed at the moment. He was about to cross the street and join them, but hesitated when he saw that there was a third member of their group. He was a tall man with a squared chin and white hair that was shaved down into a buzz cut. Domo remembered seeing the albino once before when he'd been uptown with Buda, but didn't know his name and never bothered to ask. At first he thought the white haired man might've been there to deliver the cocaine Buda had promised, but from the way L.A. and Raheem seemed to be hanging on his every word said he was no simple courier. Domo's friends were so engrossed in what he was saying that they never even noticed him slip back into his car and pull off.

Domo hit the Garden State Parkway and started driving south. He didn't have a particular destination, he just felt like he needed to keep moving. Focusing on the road was the only thing keeping him from being swallowed by the feeling paranoia that had been eating at him all night. Vita and the others pulling a no-show was unsettling to say the least. He'd hit her phone twice more since he arrived back to New Jersey, getting the voice mail both times. A part of Domo told him to leave it alone, and count his blessings that he'd avoided whatever may or may not have been waiting for him inside that warehouse, but something about it wasn't sitting right with him. He needed answers and she was the best person to give them to him.

Since he'd first gotten down with them Vita had been the one who planned the capers and she was a stickler for details, so it was impossible for her to have sent him the wrong address by accident. That so why the ruse? Was foul play in the works, or had something happened? As he thought on it deeper she had been acting strange lately. Initially he thought her behavior had been attributed to the loss of Diamonds, but he sensed there was something more to it . . . something she wasn't saying and it had been nagging at him.

About an hour after his last call to Vita, Buda started blowing his phone up and sending him texts. "Where the fuck are you?" was the gist of most of the messages. He started to call him back but decided against it. Partially because he wasn't sure where his relationship with the crew currently stood, but also in part that he wasn't sure if he was ready to hear whatever Buda had to say. What if something had happened to Vita because he hadn't been there to watch their backs? Domo felt like a sucker for the thought. For all he knew Vita could've been trying to lure him to his death and he was more concerned about her than himself. Good pussy could screw a man's mind up worse than drugs.

By the time Domo tired of driving up and down the Parkway it was nearly daybreak, and he had burned up an entire tank of gas. He'd contemplated grabbing himself a hotel room for the night rather than face his mother, but he reasoned that putting it off would only delay the inevitable. It was time to face the music so he headed home. As Domo stepped through the small white gate in front of his apartment unit, he felt the hairs on his arm stand up. He looked up and down the street and didn't see anyone. His foot had just touched the steps of his front porch when he heard movement on the side of the house. Drawing his gun, he moved cautiously to investigate. It was then that he saw someone shambling towards him from the shadows of his backyard.

"Blood, you picked the wrong house to rob," Domo hissed, chambering a round into his pistol. The figure ignored the threat and kept advancing. Domo's finger tightened on his trigger, but he paused when Vita stepped into view. She looked worn and was limping, with a gun dangling from her hand. "V, don't make me do something stupid out here. Drop your strap!" He aimed the pistol at her head.

Vita let out what he could only assume was a chuckle, before tossing her gun to the ground. "Chill out, pretty boy. I've been shot once tonight and it's overrated," she said before collapsing into his arms.

Diamonds found himself in a world of pain. Blue and Tariq had been beating the hell out of him for most of the night. Every time he felt like he was going to die, they would stop to let him wallow in his pain until they got their second winds, before starting in again. It was as Blue had promised, his death wouldn't be painless nor quick. One of his eyes was closed and his jaw felt like it was hanging off the hinges, but he was beyond the point of pain. He just wanted it to be over.

"This sure is a tough son of a bitch, huh Blue?" Tariq said as they drug Diamonds up the stairs and out into the morning air. They stopped sort of the railing overlooking the water near the foot of the statue.

"Tougher than I expected," Blue agreed, as he knelt at Diamonds' feet and began wrapping a length of chain around them. "He'd have made a better recruit than fish food, but that ain't our call."

"Think we should work him over a little more before we dump him?" Tariq asked anxiously.

"Nah, man. I think he's suffered enough. Let's just get this over with," Blue told him. He and Diamonds were on two different sides of the battle lines, but in his short time knowing him he had come to respect the bandit king. Most men would've folded within the first day or so of what they had put him through, but Diamonds had endured it for a week and never once broke.

"Yeah, I guess you're right." Tariq propped Diamonds against the safety rail overlooking the ocean below. It was at least a twenty-foot drop. "Say, what do you think will kill him first, hitting the rocks or being dragged away by the current?" he joked.

"Stop being a dick and help me get him over," Blue told him. They were just about to dump Diamonds into the bay when they heard footsteps crunching on the gravel behind them. "Show yourself!" Blue ordered.

"Easy fellas, it's just me." Minister appeared from the shadows with his hands held high.

"Man, you almost got plugged creeping up on us like that." Blue holstered his gun. "I thought you went into the city with Slim and Rolling?"

"I was supposed to, but me and this brother have some unfinished business." Minister nodded at Diamonds. "You don't mind, do you?"

"Not at all." Blue stepped back. "But if you plan on working him over for a time then it'll be on you to get rid of the body. We're ready to punch out."

"Disposing of bodies is my specialty." Minister smiled and turned his attention to Diamonds.

"So, you come to get your pound of flesh too, yeah?" Diamonds mustered a smile. If he was going to die he'd rather it had been at the hands of an honorable man like Minister rather than Slim's two shit-head goons.

"Nah, man. I lack the cruel streak shared by my comrades. I'll make this quick." Minster drew his gun and placed it to Diamonds' forehead. "Can I ask you something?"

"Seeing how you the one with the gun, I don't see why not," Diamonds replied.

"Your boy you were telling me about, Rasul, do you think you'll see him in the afterlife?"

Diamonds weighed the question. "I strongly doubt it. Rasul was a good dude at heart, but me not so much. I think we'll be moving in two different directions on that stairway to eternity."

"Man, you gonna handle your business or keep asking dumb ass questions?" Tariq snapped. He was ready to be rid of Diamonds once and for all. In response to his question Minister turned his gun on Tariq and shot him once in the head.

"What the fuck are you doing?" Blue asked in shock.

"Hopefully, the right thing," Minister said before putting two bullets into Blue.